"Mandy who?"
The man glared at her

His expression and manner of speaking announced very clearly that she had no right to be there.

"Mason," she said. "I'm—er—I'm a relative of Mrs. Fernham."

"I've never heard of you. Precisely what relation are you to Dorothy Fernham?"

"Actually," she said awkwardly, "it's rather hard to explain."

"I bet it is." He glared at her again. "You'd better come up to the house."

He didn't know—surely he couldn't know? Maybe he imagined she was a burglar casing the joint—though she hardly looked like one, sitting on the lawn with sketching pad in hand. She'd just have to persuade him that he was wrong—before he found out the truth.

English author **SALLY COOK** lives in Norwich with her two small sons. She has been a professional writer for nine years, but only recently has branched into fiction. This is her second appearance in the Harlequin Presents line.

Books by Sally Cook

HARLEQUIN PRESENTS
1223—DEEP HARBOUR

Don't miss any of our special offers. Write to us at the following address for information on our newest releases.

Harlequin Reader Service
901 Fuhrmann Blvd., P.O. Box 1397, Buffalo, NY 14240
Canadian address: P.O. Box 603,
Fort Erie, Ont. L2A 5X3

SALLY COOK

belonging

Harlequin Books

TORONTO • NEW YORK • LONDON
AMSTERDAM • PARIS • SYDNEY • HAMBURG
STOCKHOLM • ATHENS • TOKYO • MILAN

Harlequin Presents first edition August 1990
ISBN 0-373-11287-4

Original hardcover edition published in 1989
by Mills & Boon Limited

Printed in U.S.A.

CHAPTER ONE

MANDY MASON sucked the end of her pencil, and gazed thoughtfully at the scene in front of her.

She was sitting on the very edge of a smooth expanse of lawn that swept down to the waters of Catwood Broad, one of the smallest and least well-known of the Norfolk Broads. Among the reeds that bordered the broad, a family of moorhens were playing chase, and far out across the water, silhouetted against the willows and alders on the far shore, was the triangular white sail of a small yacht.

How still the light was, she thought. It would be difficult to capture that peculiar quality in a pencil drawing: she might do better to try a watercolour when she got back to her flat. She scribbled a note down the side of her paper, and then began to block out the main features of the view.

It was a job that demanded all her concentration, for the scenery was quietly pleasing rather than dramatic, and she found it difficult to work out how to do justice to it. She licked the tip of her pencil, and with the blackened lead she began to sketch the outline of a willow tree.

A shadow fell over her paper just as she was marking the bold vertical of the trunk. How annoying. The sky had seemed a cloudless blue when she had sat down, but it was one of those English spring days when the weather could change with alarming speed. She glanced upwards, and twisted her head round to look for the sun.

Between her and its unclouded light was standing a man. A tall man, standing very close to where she sat, so that the dense shadow he cast fell right across her and her drawing-board.

Mandy jerked backwards, and dropped her pencil in her confusion. Before she could recover it had rolled down the steep slope of smooth, short grass, and fallen with a plop into the water among the reeds.

'Curse it!' she exclaimed.

'Here, let me get it.'

The man had no need to push her out of the way: she moved aside instinctively as he paced forwards and bent down to look into the water. He knelt, reached out a large hand, and a moment later turned back to her, brandishing a wet pencil.

'Er—thanks,' said Mandy, taking it from him.

The little interruption had given her time to get her thoughts together, and her mind now seemed to be working at alarming speed. She had been so sure the house was empty. Mr Fernham was at his yard, the barmaid in the pub back in Little Catwood village had told her, and Mrs Fernham had gone to London for a hospital appointment. Neither of them was due back for hours. And she knew nobody else had been there when she arrived, because she had knocked on the front door several times, *and* walked round the back and called out.

But there was definitely someone else there now: a very large someone, staring at her with an intensity that she found extremely disconcerting. His look was penetrating, but it wasn't at all friendly.

It came to Mandy, even more uncomfortably, that she had absolutely no right to be sitting on the lawn of Heron's Nest. As for the man who was staring at her—well, whoever he was, his look and his manner announced very clearly that he had every right to be there, and every right to demand to know—as he was doubtless just about to do—what on earth she was doing there.

Mandy opened her mouth, and shut it again. Then she opened it again, with more determination, and said, holding out her right hand, from which she had just transferred the pencil, 'How do you do? I'm Mandy Mason.'

'Grant Livingstone,' said the man, taking her hand. Then he seemed to recall that this wasn't the approach he had intended, and he added, more brusquely, 'Mandy *who*?'

'Mason. I'm—er—I'm a relative of Mrs Fernham's.'

'Are you now?' said Grant Livingstone, consideringly. 'I've never heard of you,' he went on, in a more accusing tone.

'I can't say I've ever heard of you either,' Mandy retorted sharply. She picked up her drawing-board, and got to her feet. 'I came to visit, but it seems the Fernhams aren't at home, so I thought I'd just do a quick couple of sketches of the broad before I went. Save a complete waste of a day,' she added, by way of further explanation.

'You didn't think to phone before calling in?'

'Obviously not. I—I wasn't sure I'd get this far today, and I didn't want to make an appointment and then disappoint them.' She smiled. She was rather proud of this piece of quick thinking. 'But now you're here,' she went on, with growing recklessness, 'perhaps I could beg a cup of tea before I push off.'

This was a mistake, she realised as soon as the words were out. Grant Livingstone was looking at her as if he could hardly credit her boldness. More, he too was on his feet now, and her temporary height advantage had been very firmly wiped out.

Heavens, was he *tall*, she thought, as her eyes travelled upwards and upwards before connecting with his. She was a willowy five foot eight herself, and it wasn't often she came across men who made her feel small. Grant Livingstone was surely six foot five or even six foot six, and solidly built with it.

His size alone would have been reason enough for the butterflies that flickered in her insides: the sheer bulk of him was intimidating. But it wasn't this that set Mandy's alarm bells ringing: it was the firm set of his jaw, the straight line of his mouth, and above all the unwavering directness of the look he had fixed on her, all of which told her that this wasn't a man to be tangled with lightly.

His eyes aren't brown, she noticed, inconsequentially; they're more a hazel colour, with little brown and yellow flecks. And his hair has a reddish tinge where the sun strikes it. He'd be a good man to paint. Not in watercolours, though: it would need the richness of oils to do justice to his colouring.

'Precisely what relation are you to Dorothy Fernham?'

Mandy jumped out of her reverie, and landed firmly back on the ground.

'Actually,' she said awkwardly, 'it's rather hard to explain.'

'I bet it is.' Grant Livingstone glared at her. 'You'd better come up to the house.'

He waved across the lawns towards it. A cup of tea, after all? Mandy knew as soon as she thought it that that wasn't what he was suggesting. An interrogation would be more like it. And that wasn't a pleasant thought, because she had the impression that, if Grant Livingstone set his mind to finding something out, it wouldn't be easy to stop him.

He didn't know—he surely couldn't know? No, he couldn't. It wasn't as if anybody had been expecting her to arrive at Heron's Nest. No, he must suspect something quite different. Maybe he even imagined she might be a burglar casing the joint, though she could hardly have looked much like one, sitting on the lawn, sketching the broad. That was all right; she could surely persuade him easily enough that he was wrong there. But she couldn't, *mustn't* let him find out the truth.

'After you,' he said in a firm voice.

Mandy managed a trembling smile. 'Thanks,' she said, and set out across the lawn.

Heron's Nest. Such a lovely name for a house, Mandy had thought when she first heard of it. Then she had imagined a Tudor mansion, all mellow brick and mullioned windows, or perhaps a thatched cottage. In fact Heron's Nest wasn't either, but it hadn't disappointed her. It was a sturdy, rather plain-looking redbrick house—Victorian, she reckoned, or possibly Edwardian—with sash windows and a deep porch, redeemed by good proportions and by its setting, well back in its grounds, and at an angle which made the entrance visible from the drive, while giving the front rooms views down across the lawns to the waters of Catwood Broad.

The lawns were long, and it seemed to take her an eternity to cover the distance to the porch. She was acutely aware of Grant Livingstone's eyes on her: watchful, penetrating, doubtless sizing her up and trying to decide what to do about her sudden appearance.

If he had been a different man, she might have tried her feminine wiles on him: put a sway into her walk, fluttered her eyelashes, played the helpless female, too dumb to realise that she had been trespassing on private property. But Grant Livingstone unnerved her too much for her to do any of that, and there was something about his manner that told her that he'd not find it at all amusing, let alone appealing, if there was any hint that she was trying to flirt her way out of an awkward situation. Instead she speeded up a little, and made it to the relative safety of the porch several paces ahead of him.

She stepped sideways to let him to the door. He pulled a bunch of keys out of the pocket of his well-worn denims, and selected the right one from the dozen or so without hesitation. He turned it firmly in the lock, then pushed the door open and stood aside to let Mandy into the house.

She walked into a hall, large and rather square, with three or four doors leading off it, and a heavy oak staircase leading upwards. There was no furniture to be seen, but the walls on either side of the stairway were solid with pictures, row upon row of them, reaching from the ceiling almost to the floor. The overall effect was cosy and relaxed and welcoming: Heron's Nest felt like a house whose owners she would like.

A thud behind her made her spin round. The front door had shut behind Grant Livingstone, and he had turned, Mandy saw, to ram home the heavy bolt at the very top of the frame. Imprisoning her? That was a melodramatic way of putting it, but his intention was obvious: he didn't intend to let her go until he had a convincing explanation of what she had been doing at Heron's Nest.

'Oh, I should have told you. I posted a . . .' Mandy moved forward towards Grant, and bent down. 'Move your foot a minute.'

'A what?' Grant demanded, without shifting an inch.

Mandy set her hand to the side of his sneaker, and gave a push. She might as well have been trying to move a rock.

'A note,' she said, with a touch of exasperation. 'You're standing on it.'

Grant bent down, and lifted his foot just far enough to feel under it. 'So I am,' he agreed grudgingly. He extracted a folded piece of drawing paper, straightened himself, and unfolded it.

Mandy could remember every word he was reading: it was barely half an hour since she had written them, and she had put a lot of thought into the short message. 'Dear Mr and Mrs Fernham,' the note said. 'I called to say hello, but unfortunately nobody was here. I'll ring you in a few days. Your relative, Mandy Mason.'

Grant Livingstone glanced up, and his hazel eyes met hers again, faintly narrowed this time.

' "Your relative",' he repeated. 'That's an odd way of describing yourself.'

'It's an odd situation,' Mandy responded. 'You see, I don't actually know what relationship I am to the Fernhams.'

'You *don't know*?' echoed Grant, in obvious disbelief.

'Honestly. I'm an amateur genealogist, you see: I've been looking into my family tree. My mother was a Blackwater, and as far as I've been able to learn, Dorothy Fernham was a Blackwater before she married too. I'm pretty sure we're cousins of some kind. It's an unusual name, you see: almost certainly all the surviving Blackwaters are related. But I haven't been able to work out exactly what the relationship is, so I thought I'd call and introduce myself, and see if Mrs Fernham could throw some light on a muddy stretch of water. Genealogically speaking,' she finished, with a tentative smile.

Grant missed this effort, because he had turned his gaze once more to the note.

'That's true,' he said thoughtfully, as if to himself. 'Dorothy *was* a Blackwater. But then, everyone around these parts knows that.' He looked up again. 'So you got her address from the Public Records Office?'

'I found the record of her marriage in Little Catwood Church, and that told me her present name. Then I checked in the local telephone directory, and I found that there was a Fernham, J in Little Catwood, so I assumed it must be the Fernham, J that Dorothy Blackwater had married.'

'From the telephone directory? So did you telephone her?'

She hadn't, and to admit that would seem peculiar to Grant Livingstone, she realised. For a moment she thought of lying to him, and then praying that the unknown Dorothy Fernham would back her up. No, it was too much of a risk.

'To be honest, I didn't,' she said, fixing wide grey eyes on him. 'I know that must seem odd, Mr Livingstone, but I'd already fixed up this short holiday in Norfolk, you see, and it was a question of— well, fitting things in. The name of the house fascinated me. Heron's Nest is such an unusual name, and it really appealed. I was so taken with the idea of coming to see the house and meeting Mrs Fernham face to face that I didn't particularly want to have her answer my questions over the phone. I thought I'd just call in when my travels took me to Little Catwood, and explain to her then.'

Grant Livingstone's eyes held hers very steadily, even after this little explanation had trailed away. Mandy stared resolutely back. All right, she told herself, it wasn't the gospel truth: but she did have a good reason for wanting to see Dorothy Fernham, and absolutely nothing to be ashamed of.

At last Grant relented, and slowly dropped his gaze. 'I've just got to pick up some papers,' he said, 'and then I'm going back to the yard. You can follow me.' He saw the hesitation in Mandy's face, and added, 'You do have a car?'

'Oh, yes.' She had hired one specially for the trip, knowing that Little Catwood was well away from train and bus routes. 'It's parked on the verge, just beyond the drive. But I really wouldn't want to disturb Mr Fernham at work...'

'You won't be disturbing him,' Grant retorted. 'It's nearly lunch time; he'll be breaking off when I get back. I'm sure he'll be interested to have lunch with his new relative. Wait there, I'll be back in a minute.' He disappeared down the hall, and through a door at the far end.

She hardly had much alternative but to wait, Mandy thought edgily: he was doubtless listening and would hear if she tried to draw the bolt, and there was no other exit visible. And then she'd have to do as he said and go to meet Mr Fernham, or she would only fuel the suspicions he had already made only too obvious. Things could be worse, she supposed, but it wasn't what she had planned at all. She had wanted to meet Mrs Fernham, ideally in circumstances where she could tell her the truth, and not Mr Fernham, to whom she would have to lie even more convincingly than she had lied to Grant Livingstone.

She let out a sigh, and glanced around her. What a lot of pictures there were. Did Mrs Fernham paint? Perhaps it ran in the family. She was just moving closer to look at some of them when she heard heavy footsteps and saw Grant reappearing, with a folder of papers under his arm.

'The yard's in Wroxham,' he said, as he unfastened the door again. 'Do you know the road?'

Perhaps she would have a chance to lose him on it, Mandy thought with a surge of eagerness. Many of the Broadland roads were narrow and twisting, with plenty of side roads and blind bends.

'I came the other way, I think.'

'It's almost a straight road from here. But you can leave your car here if you like, and I'll bring you back afterwards.' Grant turned his head sideways, and threw her a challenging look.

No, that would mean sitting next to him for however many miles it was to Wroxham, and facing another inquisition, most likely.

'I'm sure I'll manage to follow you,' Mandy said sweetly.

'You'd better,' Grant returned. 'Catwood Wherrymen, it's called. You can park in the forecourt next to me.'

He strode off down the gravel drive, towards a Range Rover with that year's registration plates, parked just by the side of the house. Mandy stared after him. All those questions to her, she thought, annoyed, and he hadn't explained himself at all! He worked with Mr Fernham, that was evident: at Catwood Wherrymen, a boatyard presumably, since this was boating country. And he was prosperous, to judge by the car. He was very tall for a boatman. What kind of boats were they? How wonderful it would be if they really were wherries, the old Norfolk sailing barges. But that didn't seem likely if it was a commercial yard, as wherries couldn't have been used on the Broads for many years.

Her questions weren't going to be answered by staring at Grant Livingstone and his car, though, and when he had unlocked the car door he turned to check that she was following suit. She straightened her drawing-board under her arm, and set off down the drive.

Losing Grant Livingstone on the short drive was quite impossible, Mandy found: he never went above thirty miles an hour, and never overtook another vehicle. He drove through the tiny village of Little Catwood— no more than a pocket-handkerchief village green, dominated by the shadow of a high-towered medieval church, with a pub next to it, and a couple of old low houses—and then turned on to a road that was signed to Wroxham.

Mandy trailed behind his Range Rover in her hired Fiat, trying to ignore the cold feeling in the pit of her stomach. All during the journey from London to Norfolk she had told herself that she was doing the right, the only thing by going to see Dorothy Fernham, but now she couldn't help feeling that it had been quite insane of her, and it was likely to end in disaster.

If only, if only Grant Livingstone hadn't come to Heron's Nest! Then she would just have finished her sketch and gone away, and she could have phoned Mrs Fernham quietly another day. Now her visit was going to cause the sort of widespread interest she had most wanted to avoid, and, even if she managed to get through the lunch without giving herself away, she would never be able to introduce herself to Mrs Fernham in the way she had planned. Curse, curse Mr Livingstone!

At last they approached the outskirts of the little town of Wroxham, and Grant Livingstone glanced ostentatiously into his rear-view mirror, indicated left, and turned into a side road. Sighing again, Mandy followed him. There was no point in trying to escape: he would have noted her car number, and she reckoned him quite capable of going to the police if she tried to elude him now.

Ahead of them, blocking off the end of the road, was a gateway, with above it a large blue sign on which 'Catwood Wherrymen' was printed in black. Grant swung his car through the open gates, and into a parking space just on the other side. Mandy followed, and by the time she had set the handbrake on her Fiat he was waiting at her car door.

Mandy opened the door and clambered out. If she really were a distant cousin she would be looking forward to this encounter, she reminded herself; she tried a nervous smile, which Grant did not return.

'It's this way,' he said, and took her by the elbow. Their path led them down to the river: they had parked only a few yards away from it. When they came closer, though, she realised that it was not the River Bure proper, but a cutting off the main channel. Half a dozen motor cruisers were moored in a row in the still water.

She stopped to look at them, and Grant's pressure on her elbow eased, as if in acceptance of her interest.

'These are your boats?'

'Our hire fleet, yes.'

Their hire fleet. It was what she should have expected, she realised: almost every boatyard in this area would run a hire fleet of cabin cruisers. But she was oddly disappointed to see these pleasant but ordinary boats, when her mind had been fixed on the idea of the wherries after which the yard was named.

'You have a lot,' she said politely.

'These are just the spares, in case of breakdown. The main fleet is all out. We're fully booked this week.' He pulled at her again, guiding her firmly on towards the yard office, and Mandy went with him unprotestingly. She was very conscious of the large bulk of him, so close at her side. He would make an effective bodyguard, she thought momentarily; or a gaoler.

The yard office was just ahead of them, a neat, modern brick building. Grant released her arm to push open the glass door, calling out as he did so. 'James! I've brought you a visitor.'

'Oh, damn, has that Fish woman . . .' James Fernham looked up from a cluttered desk as he spoke, and then his voice trailed away. 'Who are you?'

'Recognise her?' Grant challenged.

'I'm afraid you won't,' said Mandy in a cheerful voice, resolutely ignoring Grant's interruption. 'I'm Mandy Mason. Hello, Mr Fernham.'

Mr Fernham didn't take her outstretched hand. Instead he was staring at her as if he'd seen a ghost. Then he blinked, seemed to come to his senses, and said mildly, 'I'm sorry, my dear, for a moment I took you for someone else.'

'Who else?' Grant demanded.

'What?' Mr Fernham glanced at him, still clearly disconcerted. 'Oh, you wouldn't remember her, Grant, it was before your time. Dorothy had a cousin called Frances—Frances Blackwater, and just then when this young lady came through the door I thought for a split second that it was Frances walking in. Mind, it couldn't have been, it's well over twenty years since Frances emigrated to New Zealand, and she was around your age then, my dear. She had hair like yours, though, worn in much the same style, and— well, even now when I look carefully, the resemblance is really striking.'

'That's not so very surprising,' Mandy said gently. 'My mother was a Blackwater, and as I told Mr Livingstone earlier, I'm fairly sure I'm a relative of your wife's.'

'Then that explains it,' James Fernham said with obvious relief. 'Of course you must be, it's obvious from the look of you. Mary, you said your name was?'

'Mandy. It's short for Amanda, Amanda Jean.' Mandy couldn't resist casting a glance of triumph at Grant, and it was no great surprise when it connected with his appraising look.

'I don't see the resemblance,' Grant said stubbornly. 'Maybe with this cousin, but there's nothing of Dorothy in Miss Mason.'

Mandy swallowed her retort, and made herself stand the scrutiny of the two men in silence. For a moment she wished she had worn smarter clothes for her visit, though she had chosen her outfit with care, partly for its practicality and largely because she felt comfortable and good in it. Her grey cotton shirt was years old, the cotton worn to baby softness by hundreds of washings, but the colour brought out the depths in her eyes, which she had always thought of as her best feature: large and wide-set, they dominated even her strong features. The colour was reflected too in the grey leather belt which held up her denims, and in her calf-length boots, and a splash of brighter colour was added by the red scarf she had tied round her neck.

So she looked like Dorothy Fernham's cousin? That was a strange thought: Mandy's looks were distinctive, even if they fell short of beauty, and though she drew many interested glances she had never before been mistaken for somebody else. Few people had hair like hers, milky fair and naturally so curly as to be all but uncontrollable, and it was even odder to think that this unknown Frances had worn hers in the same style, blunt-cut so that it spread in a haze that ended just above her shoulders. Presumably Frances had had a similar square-chinned face and squarish shoulders too, if the resemblance really was so striking. Presumably she was tall. Was Dorothy Fernham tall? Mandy mentally measured James Fernham, standing behind his desk. Against Grant Livingstone he seemed small, but in fact, she realised, he was close to her own height. Not tall for a man, even then, and his wife was probably at least an inch or two shorter: perhaps in this, too, Dorothy was much less like Mandy herself than her cousin was.

'There *is* a similarity in the shape of their faces,' James said at last. 'Don't you see it now, Grant?'

'A little,' Grant grudgingly conceded. 'She has something of old George Blackwater in her, I can see that.'

'Of course she has,' James agreed. 'Who was your—oh, what a pity Dorothy can't be here, she knows the family so much better than I do. But you'll join us for lunch, Miss Mason? I'm being rude keeping you standing here. Let's go out and get a bite to eat, and we can talk then. The Railway Arms, do you think, Grant?'

'Should do.'

'I'll just tell Mavis we're...' James Fernham disappeared as he spoke through the door of the adjoining office, and Mandy found herself momentarily alone again with Grant.

His eyes had barely left her, and even now they were firmly fixed on her face. It made her feel flustered. No need for it to, she told herself firmly: if he was still searching for traces of the resemblance to Dorothy and Frances and their family, then let him search. She hadn't lied about that, and, as James had already confirmed, he would find what he was looking for.

'That's fine,' said James Fernham, reappearing with a jacket in his hand. 'I told Mavis we might be a few minutes late back. Now, what are you doing in Norfolk, Mandy—you don't mind if I call you Mandy?'

'Not at all,' she said, and she meant it: she had warmed to James Fernham immediately. 'I'm just here on a short holiday, and I had especially wanted to call in and introduce myself to yourself and your wife.'

Over a sandwich lunch at the Railway Arms—a plain but pleasant modern pub just across the road from the yard—she told the rest of her story, and to her relief it went smoothly. In James Fernham's eyes her resemblance to Frances Blackwater was clearly more than enough recommendation, and fortunately he asked no questions about her family that she could not answer easily, simply saying that she would have to mull over their precise relationship with Dorothy when they had a chance to meet.

Grant Livingstone still didn't seem to be won over, though. Several times Mandy caught him staring at her, though he generally looked away when her own look challenged him. Twice he mentioned his encounter with Mandy back at Heron's Nest and, though there was nothing objectionable in his words, Mandy sensed that he was trying to stir suspicion in James. He didn't succeed, though, and by the time the conversation changed to boats Mandy had begun to relax and to enjoy herself.

'You must have a big fleet, James,' she prompted.

'Not that many,' James replied. 'We've just the four finished boats, and the one we're working on at the moment.'

'But I saw at least half a dozen cruisers in the cutting in your yard...'

'Oh, cruisers!' James said, and to her surprise Mandy heard a laugh come from Grant Livingstone. It was a warm, rich sound that matched his colouring, but it annoyed her: she had a sensation for a moment that he was laughing at her.

'James doesn't count the cruisers, Miss Mason,' he explained. 'They just pay the bills. He's talking about the real boats, the wherries.'

'The real—so you *do* have wherries!' exclaimed Mandy.

'Certainly we do,' James said. 'That's my true love, Mandy.'

'And mine.'

Grant said this with a firmness that surprised Mandy, and she glanced at him to see the expression that accompanied it, but James was already saying, 'You can't have seen the wherries, then? We'll have to show you round the *Grey Lady* when we get back to the yard.'

Grant's look shifted to James immediately, with a hint almost of warning in it. 'You're forgetting, James,' he said harshly. 'You've Foster coming at two, and he's likely to keep you busy all afternoon.'

'Damn, so he is,' James agreed. 'But you're free for a while, aren't you, Grant? I've never yet known you to refuse to show anyone over your pride and joy.'

Grant's mouth opened slightly, and for a moment Mandy thought that she was going to prove the exception to this airily stated rule. But instead he said curtly, 'I won't have long to spare.'

'Nor I, I'm afraid,' Mandy hastily added. 'I have to drive back down to London tonight, and I mustn't leave it too late setting off.'

'Oh, what a pity,' James exclaimed. 'I thought you said you were on holiday for several days.'

'I was. But this is the last of them, unfortunately.'

'Then you'll miss Dorothy.'

'Unless she'll be back very soon, I'm afraid I shall. I asked in Little Catwood, and they said she had gone to London for a hospital appointment...'

'That's right. She generally gets the three-thirty train back, so she won't reach Wroxham until half-past six or so.'

'Generally? She does this regularly?'

There had been no sign of worry about his wife in James Fernham's voice, but even so, his words had woken an uneasiness again in Mandy. Dorothy Fernham's hospital appointment had meant nothing to her when the barmaid in Little Catwood had mentioned it: she had assumed it was something trivial. But Norfolk women didn't have regular hospital ap-

pointments in London without good cause, she
thought suddenly.

'Every month or so at the moment,' James Fernham
replied. He paused, and then said in a gentle voice,
'I should warn you, Mandy. My wife suffers from
multiple sclerosis.'

CHAPTER TWO

'SORRY to leave you so soon, Mandy,' James Fernham said, as he and Mandy and Grant reached the door of the office once more. 'But you'll call Dorothy in a day or two, I hope?'

'I certainly will,' said Mandy, in a voice which managed, she hoped, to hide all the inner confusion which his revelation had caused her.

'She'll be looking forward to it.' James pushed open the door and disappeared inside.

Mandy turned and glanced at Grant. He had hardly spoken in the last half-hour or so at the pub, and she was half expecting him now to cry off from showing her his wherry. But instead he said curtly, 'It's this way,' and set off down the path that led around the end of the office building.

She followed him. The path led to a series of boatsheds that blocked the view of the river beyond. Grant paused for her to catch him up, and indicated the narrow track that led between two of the sheds. Without meeting his glance, Mandy struck out along it. She sensed him following close behind her.

A moment later she was in sight of the water: and involuntarily she let out a gasp.

The wherry looked enormous, compared to the little cabin cruisers that she had seen all over the Broads. It was about fifty feet long, all made of wood with black-tarred sides. She had expected it to have the dullness of a coal barge, but in fact it shone in the sunlight: the black was bright and dense, and the cabins were gaily painted, with blue and white sides and red tops. The huge mast had been lowered across the top of the cabins, and a heavy mass of black sail was lashed around it.

'They were fair-sized boats, the Norfolk wherries,' said Grant, as if she had spoken her thoughts out loud. 'Some were even bigger than this. The *Grey Lady* would have managed around forty tons of cargo if she'd been built as a trading ship. But she's a passenger wherry, as you can see: she has berths for twelve.'

'How strange to see a black sail,' Mandy said.

'All wherries have them, it's their trademark almost. They used to call them the black-sailed traders. We've treated the sail in the traditional way, with a mixture of seal oil and tar. And they are all very simply rigged, with just the single mast and one large sail.'

Grant's words were matter-of-fact, but his tone spoke of something else: of a passionate pride in, and love for, the vessel in front of them. Looking at the *Grey Lady*, Mandy could well understand how it might fire a man in that way. And Grant was a man who felt deeply, she sensed: a man who would commit his emotions slowly, and then hold fast to them for ever more.

As he was holding, she thought uneasily, to his first suspicions of her. Though there was warmth enough in his tone when he spoke of the wherry, there was none in the face he turned to Mandy when she said with unguarded eagerness, 'I'd love to sail in her.'

'The simple rigging doesn't make her any easier to handle. Quite the opposite, in fact. She can manage with a crew of two if needs be, but she needs a skilled sailor to skipper her.'

'I've sailed a little,' Mandy said, 'but I'd hardly call myself an expert. How do you hire her out? Could I go out with a party some time, maybe?'

'I'll check the schedules. It won't be today, though.'

'I wasn't expecting that,' she replied hastily.

'You can come on board and look at her.'

Grant strode casually across the ribbon of water that divided the *Grey Lady* from the land. Then he turned back to Mandy, and reached out a hand.

She took it, and let him draw her on to the boat. He released her hand as soon as she was safely on board, and began to show her around.

The wherry was so heavy that she didn't rock at all as they stepped about on her. Grant showed Mandy the plankway along the side of the deck, its surface roughened with tar and sawdust to give the boatmen a firm foothold for quanting, the local custom of pushing the boat along with a pole when the wind dropped. He took her into the neat fore cabin—now the wherrymaster's cabin—with its black-leaded stove and two narrow parallel bunks, and into the more spacious passenger accommodation in what would, in a trading wherry, have been the cargo holds.

Though his manner was impersonal, he didn't hurry the tour, or give Mandy any impression that he was eager to be through with it. All too soon, though, they had exhausted the delights of the cabins and emerged back on the deck. Grant turned back for a moment to make sure that she was safely up the steps from the main cabin, fastened the cover behind her, and then turned to gaze down the river. His hand caressed the bright vermilion surface of the hold cover, in an absent-minded but oddly sensuous way.

'Is this an old boat?' Mandy asked, with a sudden impatience to draw his attention back to her.

He shook his head. 'No, you don't find old wherries in a condition for restoration. You'll see plenty of hulks of sunken wherries around the Broads, but they are all decayed beyond rescuing. The *Grey Lady*'s a new copy from a Victorian design.'

'So you adapted the design and built it as a pass-enger boat?'

'We didn't need to. There have been pleasure wherries since the 1860s. This is just the way the Victorians designed her.'

'And who did the building?'

'James and I, with a bit of help from the rest of the yard staff. I did the carpentry myself, and James and I cured the sail. This is our boat through and through. I could tell you where every bolt is, where each plank came from.'

'That must be a good feeling.'

'It is,' Grant said quietly. 'We'll never make much money from her, mind,' he went on more harshly. 'But these are the boats that belong on the Broads, not those damned tin cans back there. The cruisers wreck the ecosystem, but the wherries don't. Slowly the regulations are changing as people grow more aware of conservation issues, and I reckon in twenty years time we'll have seen the end of the cruisers, and the Broads will belong to the wherries again.'

'And you'll be glad.'

'It's my dream,' Grant replied matter-of-factly.

And yet he and James Fernham ran a fleet of cruisers, Mandy thought to herself. What a complex man he was. To some those might have been the choices of a hypocrite, but she knew instinctively that Grant Livingstone was deceiving neither himself nor anyone else. He had worked out how best to bring about the state of affairs he wanted, and he was quietly and decisively setting about doing just that.

'You love it all, don't you?' she said wonderingly. 'All of this: the rivers and the broads, and the boats too.'

'It's my home,' Grant replied. 'It's where I belong.'

He stood there for a moment more, gazing downstream with a kind of absorbed contentment that made Mandy wonder for a moment if he had forgotten that she was there. Then he turned and said, with all the earlier harshness now evident once more in his voice, 'That's it, then.'

That was it. He belonged there. His life was there, his work was there: and now he wanted to get her out of the way, and let him carry on with it. He expected her to turn away and go back to the place where she belonged. Except, she thought, with a momentary rush of sheer loneliness, that she had never belonged anywhere, not in the sense that Grant seemed to belong on the wherry. She had never really known where she belonged.

She had a sudden urge to tell him the truth, to explain exactly why she had come to the Norfolk Broads and to Heron's Nest. She felt certain he would understand. He might feel that she had been wrong to come, but he wouldn't blame her for it.

But the secret she was keeping wasn't her own secret, it was Dorothy Fernham's, and she didn't have any right to tell it to anyone else, especially now she knew about Dorothy's terrible disease. She had no choice but to keep on with the lies she had been telling, and to say goodbye to Grant Livingstone knowing that the distrust he had shown her was only too well-justified. And though she had almost deceived herself for a moment into believing that she would be coming back, meeting Dorothy Fernham and taking a trip on the *Grey Lady*, she knew that she didn't have any choice about that either. She wouldn't come anywhere near Little Catwood or Heron's Nest ever again.

'Thanks for showing me round,' she said in a voice that was suddenly less steady than she had expected it to be. 'I'll make my own way back to the car.'

Grant hesitated for a moment, then he said, 'James didn't take your phone number. You'd better give it to me.'

For what? she thought bitterly. She wouldn't be phoning Dorothy Fernham: she couldn't, now. And she didn't want Dorothy Fernham to phone her either.

'There's no need.'

'James doesn't like Dorothy to worry. She'll be happier if she knows she needn't wait for you to phone.'

She needn't wait, thought Mandy; there's no need for her to wait, because I'll never phone. Then she thought: Grant Livingstone knows that. He doesn't know why, but he senses it, and that's why he's so determined to get my number.

Already he had pulled a diary from his back pocket, and was hunting out a biro to go with it. 'You can write it here,' he said, putting the diary down on the hold cover and spreading it open at a back page. 'It's quite steady.'

Mandy's hand was rather less steady, as she nervously wrote down her name and her telephone number.

'And your address,' Grant prompted.

She wrote that down too. Grant waited until she had finished, then he said curtly, 'Thanks,' tucked both diary and biro away, and in an unexpectedly sudden and fluid motion, jumped off the wherry deck and on to the shore. 'Here,' he said, 'take my hand and jump.'

Mandy jumped. Her foot slipped a little as she landed, and Grant caught at her, pulling her upright again. For just a moment she felt his strength enfolding her, and sensed the warmth of his body through the thick blue shirt he was wearing.

'Watch it,' he said, releasing her quickly. 'It can be slippery on the bank.'

She gave an awkward giggle. 'Sorry about that.'

'It's OK.'

They walked in silence back to the office. 'I won't disturb James again,' she said, 'but do thank him for lunch and everything.'

'I will.'

There was nothing else to say, but Grant hesitated for a moment before going in. Their eyes met, and for a moment Mandy felt a sharp pang of regret that she was not going to see him again. She turned away quickly, and made her way alone back to her car.

*   *   *

Nine o'clock. Mandy quickly gulped the last of her cup of coffee, and made her way from the tiny kitchen of her flat into her bedsitting-room. It was time to work.

The room was large and high-ceilinged, and a clear north light filtered through the big window and on to Mandy's drawing-board. She had dumped her drawing things on the floor the previous evening on her return from Norfolk. She unpacked them methodically, resharpened her pencils, and flicked open her sketchpad.

There was only the one sketch of Catwood Broad, and even that was unfinished. But it had the outlines she needed, and she'd worked out on the journey back to London exactly how to get the effect she wanted in a series of watercolours based on the scene. She would mix the paint thickly, and let it bleed slightly into a semi-porous sheet of paper. The fluid outlines would need to be formed by the paint itself, without pen or pencil lines to add definition. Watercolour wasn't the easiest medium but, handled really well, it had a luminous quality, and that was what she wanted, to give the impression of the way the light interacted with the water.

The colours mattered most. She had to get those right, the subtly blended shades of green and grey and blue. She pinned a new sheet of paper to her board, filled her waterpot, located a dozen clean brushes, and set to work.

By lunch time half a dozen impressionistic watercolours of the broad were drying about the room. It was one of the best morning's work she could remember. But if only, Mandy mourned to herself, she had been able to sketch the end of the broad, further beyond the house, or had had time to fix the outline of the willows more precisely. She would have loved to go back to Heron's Nest and do a much more thorough job; but there was no doubt about it, she was never going back.

She was determined not to weaken and telephone Dorothy Fernham or her husband, but she knew it was possible that Dorothy might be intrigued by the story James and Grant had had to tell, and ring her. If she did, Mandy had decided, then she would have to put her off. A new piece of evidence on her family tree would conveniently have turned up in that morning's post, proving beyond doubt that in spite of the chance resemblance to Frances Blackwater, she couldn't be any but a very distant relation of Dorothy and her family. If Dorothy insisted even then on inviting her to return to Heron's Nest, she would make an excuse and explain that her work commitments would make it quite impossible for her to come to Norfolk for many months—by which time, she hoped, the whole incident would have been forgotten.

How stupid of her it had been to give Grant Livingstone her real address and phone number. If she had thought up a false one there would have been no danger of Dorothy Fernham ringing. It had been weakness, pathetic weakness, to write it down for him. She just hadn't been able to resign herself quickly and fully enough to the depressing fact that the interlude was over even before it had begun. But it was, it was: now she was determined, and there would be no going back.

As soon as the watercolours were dry, she told herself, she would take them down to Walt's gallery and ask him to try and sell them for her. She was confident that he would: he owed her a favour, and they were good, very good. She wouldn't even keep a single painting for herself. She didn't want anything to remind her of Heron's Nest and its occupants.

Four days later, the telephone rang. Mandy was at her drawing-board, working hard on some pen-and-ink book illustrations.

She was feeling bright and cheerful. Walt had sold two of her Norfolk watercolours almost immediately, and she had plenty of other work in hand. Decently paid work, too: with her share of the money for the watercolours she had a healthy bank balance for once, and could reckon to keep on at her artwork for a while yet before she had to rush back to the temp agency for a stint of clerical work. Perhaps, after so many false starts, her career as a commercial artist was really starting to take flight.

It would be Jim on the phone, she thought—the author of the children's book she was illustrating. She rushed out to the hallway to answer the call, paint-brush in hand.

'Mandy Mason,' she said in a merry voice.

'Ah, Mandy. I'm so glad I've caught you in.'

It was a woman's voice. Mandy didn't recognise it. That was unusual: she was good at voices, and her work generally came from friends and acquaintances, not out of the blue from strangers. 'I usually am,' she said. 'Can I help you at all?'

'It's Dorothy Fernham calling.'

Mandy almost dropped the receiver. Her initial apprehension about the Fernhams had faded when a couple of days had gone by without any call: she had become convinced that there wouldn't be one, after all.

She tightened her grip and took a deep breath. 'Oh, Mrs Fernham. How nice of you to ring me. I had thought of phoning you, but I didn't want to put you to any inconvenience.'

'It's no inconvenience. Far from it, I'm full of curiosity. James told me about your visit, and I've spent all weekend trying to work out whose daughter you might be. He couldn't remember if you'd mentioned: what was your mother's name?'

'I don't think I did mention it, Mrs Fernham. In fact it was—er, Beth. Beth Blackwater. That was her maiden name, of course. She married Bert Mason, so now she's Mrs Mason. Mason's my own name: Amanda Jean Mason.'

'Beth? So your mother was christened Elizabeth? That's an unusual name for a Blackwater.'

'Is it, Mrs Fernham? I hadn't realised—in fact, I'd assumed it was a common name in the family. But then, perhaps my mother came from an entirely different branch of the family from yours,' Mandy improvised desperately.

'Oh, no,' Dorothy Fernham said firmly. 'All the Blackwaters are closely related. Tell me, what were Beth's parents' names?'

'Er—Philip and Eliza, I believe.'

There was a silence at the other end of the telephone. That made Mandy feel even more uncomfortable. Supposing there really had been a Philip and

Eliza Blackwater? There couldn't have been, she told herself. It would be the most colossal coincidence if the names she'd hit on at random were the right ones.

Then Dorothy Fernham said, in a very low voice, 'You're Susannah.'

'Susannah? I'm sorry, I don't follow you, Mrs Fernham.'

'Oh, yes, you do,' the voice persisted. 'You're my Susannah. My daughter. My daughter Susannah.'

Mandy's insides seemed to dissolve. She felt hollow inside. Susannah. Susannah Blackwater.

'Are you there?' the voice on the telephone repeated, almost panicky by now. 'Susannah, are you there?'

Mandy's hand, holding the receiver, felt curiously disembodied. She heard a voice that hardly seemed to be her own, saying very gently, 'Yes, I'm here.'

When Dorothy Fernham rang off, it was all fixed. By the middle of the following week Mandy would have finished her book project. She would travel up to Little Catwood on the Friday, and stay for a week with the Fernhams.

What else could she have done? She had been wanting to meet her real mother for months, years even. The news of Dorothy's illness had made her feel that it wasn't right to disrupt her mother's life by explaining who she was, but she hadn't had to do that: Dorothy had guessed for herself. And Dorothy wasn't merely willing to meet her: she had sounded desperately anxious for Mandy to come back to Heron's Nest.

'Come home,'—that was what Dorothy had said. It had scrunched up Mandy's heart to hear those words. Maybe that wasn't fair on Beth and Bert Mason. They had both of them done their best to make her a part of their family, but increasingly throughout her teens she had come to feel like a cuckoo in their nest. The Masons were both small, neat people, who had seemed unnerved as Mandy grew up to dwarf them. They had never appreciated her carefully thought-out jumble-sale outfits, or her longing for a career as an artist. After eighteen years of living in their house, Mandy had never had that feeling of belonging that she had sensed instantly when she'd arrived at Heron's Nest.

It was the little things she craved. How wonderful she had felt when James Fernham had pointed out a real family resemblance, after years when people who didn't know she was adopted had sometimes pretended to see a non-existent resemblance between herself and Beth. How wonderful it would be to live— even for a short week—in a house with paintings on the walls and a glorious view from the windows. How wonderful it would be to talk of aunts and uncles, grandparents and second cousins, and know that all these people shared her own heritage, and many of them even looked a little bit like her.

And how awful, a hard voice of reason reminded her, to continue to lie to James Fernham and to Grant Livingstone. For this was one point on which Dorothy had been adamant: that though Mandy Mason was very welcome to return to Heron's Nest, Susannah Blackwater was not. Apparently Dorothy had never told her husband about the daughter she had given up for adoption nineteen years earlier, and she was not prepared to confess her secret now.

Mandy had protested, but not too hard; if those were the only terms on which she was welcome to Heron's Nest, then she was prepared to accept them. And Dorothy had done her best to reassure her, promising to send her plenty of background information so that she could make her story totally convincing.

They had agreed already who Mandy should pretend to be. How fortunate it was that James Fernham should have seen such a strong resemblance between Frances Blackwater and Mandy Mason. Frances Blackwater had not been heard of since her emigration well over twenty years earlier, Mandy had now learned. Dorothy had insisted that anyone seeing her would readily believe that she was Frances's daughter, born to her and Bert Mason, the husband she had married in New Zealand, and then brought back to England as a baby by Bert and his second wife, Beth.

Anyone? Mandy had had her doubts, and expressed them. But there was no one with any cause or reason to question her story, Dorothy had reassured her. Dorothy's own parents were dead, and so were Frances's; though there were a number of other relatives living in Norfolk, none of them would be in a position to contradict Dorothy's assertions. Mandy had wanted to mention Grant Livingstone but, for reasons that she hardly dared to consider too carefully, she had not spoken his name.

She sat down on her bed, and shook out the contents of the buff card folder that she normally kept in the bottom drawer of her desk. 'My family', she had labelled it, years before, in a schoolgirl's ambitious copperplate script. It held a small selection of photos of the Mason family that her adoptive parents had given her, and a large pile of letters and papers she had accumulated in the months since she had begun the long, painful search for her real mother.

Time to change it. Time to turn it into the folder of a Mandy Mason who, like her, had had a long-standing interest in discovering her family tree; a Mandy Mason who was the daughter of Bert Mason and Frances Blackwater.

CHAPTER THREE

MANDY caught a train to Norwich two hours before the one Dorothy had recommended. All her enthusiasm for seeing Heron's Nest again and meeting Dorothy hadn't completely put her at ease about pretending to be somebody she was not for a week, and she was a little apprehensive at the thought that someone might catch her out. She wanted to make sure that her cover story would be as thorough as it possibly could be.

She felt now that it had been rather stupid of her to tell Grant Livingstone and James Fernham that she had spent several days' holiday in Norfolk, though it had made sense at the time: she had thought they would find it odd if she admitted she had come so far on a day trip. She hadn't liked lying, though, and her conscience pricked her now, making her worry that even this relatively harmless fib might trip her up.

It couldn't, she reckoned, if she took trouble to prepare some back-up for her story. She had worked out already how she might do that. A quick visit to the Tourist Information Centre in Norwich and a flick through their brochures would give her the name of a cheap hotel where she could pretend to have stayed, and a chance to check that the imaginary itineraries she had worked out for each day of her 'holiday' were realistic.

That would surely be good enough, she told herself. True, Grant Livingstone had been unnervingly suspicious when she'd first met him at Heron's Nest, but then he had had reason to be. He had no reason to suspect her now, though, not when both Dorothy and James had accepted her as a member of their family. She was probably being over-cautious in imagining he might question her at all. Certainly he would hardly go farther than a few sly questions, and she was fairly confident that her homework would make her able to handle those.

Back from the Information Centre, she grabbed a quick hamburger at the station buffet, and then tracked down the Cromer train that would take her to Wroxham. She found a window seat in a half-empty carriage, and sat back to look at the Norfolk countryside flying past.

The rickety diesel train chugged past the gardens of Wroxham's houses, over. a bridge—below her, Mandy glimpsed boatyards and a river crowded with holiday cruisers—and into Wroxham station. The station, at the edge of the small town, was very quiet. Mandy gathered together her things, handed in her ticket, and walked from the platform to the booking hall.

There, leaning against the wall and surveying the few passengers who had alighted at Wroxham, was Grant Livingstone. His gaze settled on Mandy, and her walk seemed to lose all its rhythm for a moment, until her feet gave up and stranded her in the middle of the booking hall.

Grant eased himself off the wall, and walked slowly over to her. He stopped very close to her, so close that she thought for a moment that he was going to touch her. He was wearing denims again, and a red T-shirt which did little to hide a muscular chest and a pair of hairy, lightly tanned arms.

He was not looking particularly pleased to see her.

Mandy gulped, and to her intense annoyance her portfolio began to slide out from under her arm.

'Watch it,' Grant said. He reached out and grabbed the front corner of it. 'Here, let me take that bag before you drop everything.'

She helplessly surrendered the heaviest of her two bags to him, and tightened her grip on the portfolio with her newly empty hand. Grant reached for her second bag too, and after a moment's rather undignified tussle with the strap she released that to him as well.

'Is this all the stuff you've brought?'

'Of course it is. I'm only staying for a week.'

'The car's this way.'

He turned and strode off. Mandy stared after him for a moment, then came to her senses and followed him.

Dismay was her strongest feeling; that, and a strange hollowness in the pit of her stomach. She had spent most of the journey telling herself that she wasn't likely to see him at all, and there he was, meeting her off the train. Why hadn't James Fernham come? she thought, annoyed. He would have looked pleased to see her, while Grant hadn't even pretended to welcome her back to Norfolk.

By the time she reached the station forecourt he had already opened the back of the Range Rover, and stowed the two bags inside. He held out a hand for her portfolio, and she handed it over and let him prop it up behind the bags. Then he walked round to unlock the front of the car, and waited to see her into the passenger seat. His politeness only seemed to point up his distaste at seeing her again, but Mandy forced herself to thank him, and to smile as he closed the door on her.

They drove in silence through the busy streets of Wroxham, and out on the main road that led in the general direction of Little Catwood.

Mandy's mind seemed to be working at fast-forward. She hadn't imagined his hostility, she was sure; his silence now only confirmed it. But why? Whatever he had thought when he first saw her at Heron's Nest, he had plenty of evidence by now that the story she had told him checked out. He should have been laughing off his suspicions, and instead he seemed to have become entrenched in them. Or was it just her own nervousness that was making her think so? Maybe he hadn't wanted to break his working day and come to fetch her, and he was simply resentful because the unwelcome chore had been foisted on him.

She searched her mind for a suitable remark to break the oppressive silence, and at last she said, 'Is Mrs Fernham back at the house?'

'Yes. She meant to come with me, but she's having one of her bad days.'

'Oh, I'm sorry. Does her condition vary much?'

'Quite a bit.' Grant cast her a sharply focused glance. 'There's no cure for multiple sclerosis, you probably know, but there are periods of remission. Then there are relapses, and each time it gets a little worse. Dorothy will never walk again; she'll never even drive a car. But on good days she can sit downstairs and read, or even write letters.'

'She wrote to me,' Mandy said. 'To explain how to get here.'

'So she said.' He didn't expand on this, and she gave up the attempt to keep the conversation going. They went on for several minutes in dead silence. She wondered if she might ask to put the radio on, or a cassette; there was a pile of tapes, a pleasant mixture of classics and soft rock, in front of her, but she thought he might think her pushy if she suggested playing one of them.

She tried again.

'Is Mr Fernham at the yard? Is he busy today?'

'He's gone to Yarmouth on business.'

'Thank you for coming to fetch me.'

'My pleasure.' He set it in a neutral tone, but with a coldness that wounded more than open sarcasm would have done.

They drove on in silence again. Then there was a sudden jerk, a squeal of the brakes, and the Range Rover jolted to a stop by the roadside.

Mandy had to put her hand out quickly to stop herself from falling forward.

'Sorry about that,' Grant said. 'You OK?'

'Just about.' She looked around. They were on a featureless stretch of road with hedges at either side. There were no other cars in sight, either in front of them or behind them. Why on earth had he stopped so suddenly?

Grant was reaching under the dashboard. There was a click, and the car bonnet sprung free in front of them.

'What's up?'

'Overheating,' he said tersely. 'Didn't you notice?'

No, she hadn't. She wasn't the kind of a passenger who drove by proxy; she had never even glanced at the dashboard instruments, and she hadn't taken in the implications of the changing engine pitch. She stared helplessly at the temperature gauge—falling now, but still in the red danger zone—as Grant walked round to the front of the car, hitched up the bonnet, and disappeared behind it.

He reappeared a moment later, and strode to the back of the car. He rummaged for a few minutes among the contents of a box of tools. 'Damn,' he said.

'Missing something?' she asked, twisting round in the front seat to see what he was doing.

He glanced over at her. 'It's the fanbelt. I reckon I managed to stop before it wrecked the pistons, but I don't seem to have a spare.'

'Oh.' Mandy's own acquaintance with car engines was limited to topping up the oil occasionally. She said tentatively, 'Is there a garage round here, or...?'

Grant greeted this suggestion with a look that only just fell short of open contempt. 'Back in Wroxham. There's nothing else this side of Stalham. Are you wearing tights?'

'Am I what?'

'Wearing tights. I could use them, if you are.' He slammed the back of the car, walked round to the side, and wrenched open the front passenger door. A bad-tempered gaze raked down Mandy, from her white silk blouse to her blue cotton skirt to her long legs.

She was wearing tights; it was still May, and not warm enough to go barelegged in comfort.

'Take them off. I won't look.'

'You want me to do what?'

'Take them off. Or would you like me to do it for you?' A hard hand reached out for her wrist, and virtually yanked her out of the car.

'Get your hands off me!'

'Damn well help me, and I'll be only too glad to.' He released her wrist abruptly, and strode off towards the back of the car.

She rubbed her wrist, and stared balefully at Grant's back. What a time for this to happen! She had heard of people using a pair of tights as a makeshift fanbelt, but it had always sounded like a stupid joke, not like something she might need to do herself one day. And as for peeling her tights off in front of Grant Livingstone, even with his back turned . . .

It suddenly struck her that Grant liked the idea even less than she did. It must be a nightmare for him, she thought, with a wicked sense of amusement: corralled into giving her a lift, and now stranded with her on a desolate road miles from any sign of habitation! And forced into making a suggestion she was clearly only too likely to take in the wrong way! A very inappropriate smile turned up the corners of her mouth.

'Get on with it,' Grant's harsh voice muttered.

It was almost a pity to spoil the fun, but common sense got the better of her naughtier inclinations. 'I've a couple of spare pairs in my bag,' she called out.

He turned promptly, his face transformed by his evident relief into something almost approaching warmth towards her. 'Then let's have them.'

Mandy went round to the back of the Range Rover, reached for and unfastened her bag, and located a brand new pair of tights which she put demurely into Grant's waiting hands. She could hear him ripping off the cellophane wrapping as he strode back to the engine. There was a short silence, then he called out, 'I need a hand.'

You've still got the one that bruised my wrist, she thought resentfully. But she curbed her retort, and went to investigate.

Grant's head was bowed under the bonnet, and he seemed to be reaching down and holding something in the greasy depths of the engine cavity. Mandy bent over next to him, being careful to keep far enough away to avoid the risk of accidental contact.

He didn't turn or acknowledge her presence, except to say, 'Your hand's smaller than mine. Reach down and see if you can catch hold of the other end.'

'Down where?' she asked dubiously. 'You'll have to spell it out. Engines aren't my thing.'

'That gap there.'

He called that a gap? Somewhere in the midst of the murky mess of metal parts, covered in oil and grime, there was a very small hole, but she could hardly believe that she could be expected to put her hand through it.

'It's impossible.'

'No, it isn't. Roll your sleeve up first.'

At least that was sensible advice. Mandy straightened up, rolled her sleeve as high as it would go, bent down again, and dutifully groped in the depths of the car innards. On her second attempt she managed to grab something that felt like nylon.

'Now what?'

'Pull it back and give it to me.'

She pulled, trying to ignore the very uncomfortable sensation of hot metal scraping down her forearm. Her hand emerged, with one end of the tights still in it. She handed it over, with a triumphant grin that Grant did not appear to notice. He tied a swift, efficient knot, pulled a few times to check the tension of the makeshift fanbelt, then nodded, and slammed down the bonnet.

Mandy gave her arm a rueful glance. There were long black streaks of grease almost up to the elbow, and she had a suspicion that one of them was hiding a graze.

'I've a cloth in the back,' Grant said. 'I can get rid of the worst of that for you.'

It rather surprised her that he had noticed; he had a great deal more grease on him than she did, and she'd had a suspicion that he would expect her to stay mucky until they reached Heron's Nest. She followed him round to the back of the car, and watched him sort out a fairly large though none too clean rag from among the contents of an efficient-looking toolbox.

'Here.'

He reached for her hand before she could protest, and held it firmly trapped in one of his, while with the cloth in his other hand he proceeded to rub at the marks on her bare arm.

Mandy opened her mouth to say that she could very well do it herself, but she didn't get as far as saying the words. She simply stood there and let Grant carry on. His touch was firm, but not rough; far from hurting her, it actually felt rather pleasant.

In fact, she thought to herself, he had coped very smoothly with the little crisis. All too many of her boyfriends were prone to let out a loud groan and then dash for the nearest telephone box in such situations, but Grant had known just what to do to get the car back on the road, and he had done it without any undue dramatics. Competent, that was the word for him.

'Hey,' he said in a low voice, 'you've got a graze here.'

'Just a bit of one,' she agreed, peering at her arm. An angry red patch was evident now through the remnants of the oil.

'I'm sorry about that. You can get it patched up when we get to the house.'

'I'm not going to die from it,' she snapped.

As soon as the words were out she was sorry for them. He really had seemed sympathetic, and she had reacted as if he was still being antagonistic and baiting her! His eyes lifted to hers in response to the little outburst, and for a moment their gazes connected.

It was like tapping into an electrical circuit; a jolt of sheer adrenalin flowed through her. Grant's gaze seemed to hold her rigid: she simply couldn't look away. They stared at each other in shocked recognition for a taut few seconds, then Grant abruptly turned away, saying tersely, 'That'll have to do for now. We'd better get moving. I'll have to drive slowly for the rest of the way, and Dorothy will worry herself stupid if we're too late.'

'I wouldn't want that,' Mandy managed to say, as she moved away from him and back towards her side of the car. She heard Grant slam the back shut, and a second later he had seated himself and was cautiously revving the engine.

Mandy didn't dare even to glance at him again. She hadn't yet come to terms with her awareness; it still astonished and shocked her to realise how powerfully she had reacted to him.

Sexual attraction, that was it, she told herself as prosaically as she could. She had been aware that there was something between the two of them, an undercurrent that made them acutely conscious of each other, but until then she simply hadn't seen it from that angle. She had put it down to Grant's sheer size, to his evident suspiciousness, but she hadn't thought to put it down to the basic animal sensation that bound a man and a woman together. It was unmistakable now. She wanted him, and she knew beyond doubt that he wanted her too.

It was ridiculous, absolutely ridiculous. She barely even knew Grant Livingstone. It wasn't her style to react strongly to strange men. She often admired their looks, yes, but never before had she experienced this sudden surge of sensation and feeling that made her ache to look and touch, and yet be terrified to do either. It couldn't be right. It had to be her nervousness at the prospect of meeting her mother for the first time that was making her over-react in this disconcerting way.

She could find a dozen reasons why she should suddenly have responded to him in such a strange way, but repeating them to herself somehow didn't take away her acute consciousness of Grant Livingstone sitting just next to her, with his eyes fixed determinedly on the road ahead of them. It was the very rigidity of that gaze, sensed rather than seen, that eventually gave her the courage to turn and look at him again.

Yes, he was big, alarmingly big. He wasn't one of those gangling men who seemed to have outgrown their strength; he was well-built, though every inch of his tall frame looked to be solid muscle rather than fat. She could see the sinews in his arms and hands as he turned the wheel. How old is he? she wondered. Thirty, thirty-five perhaps—ten or fifteen years younger than James Fernham. Is he a relative of the Fernhams? Is he a relative of mine, too? She badly wanted to know, but she didn't dare to ask him.

His hair was cut very short, but it was so thick and curly that the effect wasn't at all ugly or military: it simply emphasised the pleasing shape of his head, and his firmly chiselled profile. He was more tanned than when she had seen him before, she thought: not surprising after a fortnight of fine, hot weather. By midsummer his hair and skin would be almost the same colour, a rich dark brown with just a hint of red to it. It wasn't a colouring she had ever particularly admired before, but just then she thought it magnificent. Everything about him spoke of a powerful, healthy male animal: strong and aggressive enough to be treated with respect, but not, she reckoned, with fear. At least, she wasn't afraid of him—just of herself, and the unfamiliar sensations that seemed to be stirring her insides into jelly.

Grant glanced at her only once, as he swung the car into the drive of Heron's Nest. He drove right up the driveway, and brought the car to a cautious halt just outside the front door. He got out immediately the car had stopped, without waiting for Mandy, or saying anything at all.

Mandy followed more slowly. Grant had picked up her bags, so she took her portfolio, which was all that was left, and made her own way to the porch.

'Dorothy!' he called out, as he opened the front door. He dropped Mandy's bags in the hallway, and then made for a door to one side.

Mandy herself stopped in the hallway. From the room into which Grant had gone, she could hear a voice she recognised from her telephone conversation with her mother.

'Grant, I was getting so worried. I thought the train must have been late, or maybe Mandy had missed it at Norwich.'

'Nothing like that. We just had a little problem with the car.' Grant began to explain about the fanbelt.

Mandy set down her portfolio next to her bags. She suddenly felt acutely uneasy. It would have been bad enough walking into the room and simply facing Grant in front of a stranger. But the ordeal that faced her would be a thousand times worse than that, because Dorothy Fernham was a very special stranger: she was her own mother.

What if she didn't like Dorothy? she thought in sudden terror. What if Dorothy didn't like her?

It was too late for second thoughts. She had arrived, she couldn't go back now. She took a deep breath, and made for the doorway.

The room was a drawing-room, long and light, with a series of windows looking out over the lawns and down to the broad. The few pieces of furniture that it contained were all set around the sides: in the centre was a large bare expanse of carpet. In the middle of this Grant stood, and a couple of feet away from him a woman sat in a wheelchair.

Mandy just had a moment to look, before Dorothy turned towards the door and saw her. The older woman gave her a quick, nervous smile, then her hands moved to the wheels, and she rapidly propelled herself forwards.

'So you're Mandy,' she said. 'I'm so glad to meet you.'

Mandy automatically leaned down and reached out her hand. 'I'm very glad to be able to come, Mrs Fernham.'

'Dorothy, please.'

They went through all the formalities without stumbling, but Mandy was desperately nervous, and so, she sensed, was Dorothy. She wished Grant wasn't there watching them. His eyes never left the two of them, as Dorothy pointed Mandy to a chair, and wheeled herself over to the empty space next to it. Mandy didn't dare to look at him.

And she had to work hard to stop herself staring at Dorothy. This was her mother, she thought, amazed that the encounter she had longed for had finally happened.

As she had already known from Grant and James's comments, their physical resemblance was very slight. Dorothy's hair and skin were both darker than her own, she saw: her hair was nearer fawn than the pale gold of Mandy's, and her eyes were an even deeper grey. Dorothy's hair, like hers, was cut in a longish bob, but where Mandy's flew wild Dorothy's hung neatly to her shoulders. The older woman looked to be shorter and slighter in build too, though she did have the strong Blackwater jaw, the most prominent feature in a pleasant, rather ordinary face.

The surprise was that she looked so young. Mandy had been imagining somebody like Beth, comfortably middle-aged, but there was nothing middle-aged about Dorothy Fernham. She was slim, and only a few lines around her eyes revealed that she must be nearer forty than thirty. Her clothes were young in style, too: a simple wide-collared pink blouse and dark blue skirt that wouldn't have looked out of place on any of Mandy's friends, though they weren't as emphatically stylish as most of Mandy's own outfits.

Dorothy looked at Mandy too, but she did not meet her eyes, and a moment later she turned her head back towards Grant.

'Grant, darling,' she said, with a coaxing smile, 'could you possibly pour the champagne for us? It's all ready on the table.'

Mandy glanced around the room, and saw that a bottle of champagne had been set in an ice-bucket on a small table under the windows. There were three glasses alongside it.

'You weren't going to wait till James is back?'

'Oh, Grant, you know how James hates champagne. And I feel like celebrating right now.' Dorothy smiled again, a little nervously. 'Please.'

Mandy felt horribly embarrassed. The incident with Grant, and then the encounter with her mother: it had all been too much, and now she would have welcomed the most low-key reception possible, and a chance to escape as soon as she decently could, and recover some of her equanimity in private. And champagne! Surely that wasn't how people generally celebrated the arrival of a long-lost cousin. She couldn't help thinking that Grant would find it suspiciously extravagant of Dorothy.

Grant fuelled this thought by not replying to Dorothy's plea. The silence made things even worse. Mandy took a deep breath, and said as gaily as she could, 'What a lovely idea, Dorothy.'

That worked. Grant admitted defeat, and reached for the bottle.

'Mandy, help me with the glasses.'

The cork exploded out of the bottle, and the champagne fizzed out in a torrent, with Mandy, suddenly all thumbs, fumbling to get the glasses underneath the stream. With Grant's help she soon had three full glasses—and a small puddle on the table—and she took one over to Dorothy.

Dorothy took it with a smile, and a look that again somehow just eluded her eyes. She then looked straight past Mandy and at Grant, and said softly, 'To long-lost relatives.'

'Relatives,' Mandy echoed, taking an over-large sip from her glass and nearly choking.

Grant didn't say anything, then or subsequently, but Dorothy seemed so nervously eager to talk that there were no embarrassing silences. She began to tell Grant the tale she and Mandy had concocted, about poor cousin Frances and the baby she had borne in New Zealand.

The champagne fizzing down her throat seemed to make Mandy's insides even colder and more uncomfortable. She would have preferred Dorothy to talk about almost anything else. She couldn't help re-

membering how James had spoken of Frances in the
office of Catwood Wherrymen. She herself hadn't
mentioned being Frances's daughter then, and she was
convinced that Grant would find new grounds for
suspicion in this, the weakest link in their story.

It was disconcerting, too, to find Dorothy focusing
her attention so firmly on Grant. She was obviously
nervous, and Mandy tried to tell herself that this didn't
mean anything: it was just her way of handling a difficult scene. But it hurt, none the less. Mandy began
to long for Dorothy to give her one direct look, instead of a succession of little sideways glances that
always fell just short of meeting her eyes, and she
found it increasingly hard to hold back her annoyance when Dorothy called Grant 'dear' or
'darling', as she did frequently.

To Mandy, it seemed that Grant too was tense.
Though he didn't react in any way to Dorothy's en-
dearments, he didn't return them either, she noticed.
He simply listened silently and intently to her story,
and when it was finished he turned to Mandy and said
in a cool voice, 'You don't have any trace of a New
Zealand accent, Miss Mason.'

'That's hardly surprising, Mr Livingstone. My
father brought me back to England when I was barely
two years old, and I've never been back to New
Zealand since.'

'Oh, please,' Dorothy protested, 'we can't have this
"Miss Mason" and "Mr Livingstone". Grant is
almost one of the family, Mandy. And you *are* one
of the family, aren't you?'

'She certainly seems it,' Grant said tersely. He put
his champagne glass back down on the table by the

window. 'Do excuse me, Dorothy. I really must contact the garage before it closes today, and get hold of a new fanbelt for the Range Rover. Otherwise it'll be out of action until Monday.'

'Why don't you ring them from here, Grant, and then use James's workroom to clean up? You'll find something there to get the oil off. And I was hoping you'd show Mandy up to her room for me. We have a housekeeper to help me normally, Mandy, but this is her day off. I'd show you myself, but I can't get up the stairs any more.'

'I'm sure I'll be able to find my own way, if you tell me where to go,' Mandy said quickly.

'Oh, no. Grant will show you, won't you?'

'Of course,' Grant agreed. 'I'll just make that phone call, and I'll be right back.'

CHAPTER FOUR

THERE was an awkward silence after Grant left the room. Mandy was very conscious that he might come back at any moment. She didn't feel that it would be safe to change her manner towards Dorothy in any way. Anyway, she didn't know how to treat Dorothy; the other woman didn't seem like her mother, at least not yet, and it felt more comfortable, in a way, to treat her like the cousin she was pretending to be. But Mandy didn't want to lie either, and she couldn't think what she ought to say.

Eventually Dorothy broke the silence, saying, 'You're a painter, Grant said.'

'I'm an artist, yes,' replied Mandy, relieved to be guided to a safe topic. 'Actually I'm not comfortable with oil paints, so I'm not sure that I'd call myself a painter. I do a lot of pen and ink work, sometimes with colour washes, and watercolour sketches—that kind of thing.'

'I was a watercolourist myself.'

'Were you?' Almost involuntarily, Mandy glanced around the room. As in the hall and stairway, its walls were lined with pictures.

'Very few of these are mine,' Dorothy added quickly. 'My grandfather was the real artist of the family. I'm not sure I would have painted at all myself if it hadn't been for him. I went to art school, but

then I married as soon as I graduated, so I never tried
to make a living out of it.'

'Do you paint now?'

Dorothy shook her head. 'Not for years. It's not
that I'm incapable—my hands are still pretty steady,
and I can write letters without too much trouble. But
I stopped almost as soon I was told I had MS. I just
couldn't face going on with it any longer.'

Mandy gulped.

'That must have been a difficult decision.'

She had said it in a gentle voice, but Dorothy gave
her a sharp look which made her feel as if she had
said the wrong thing, or at least said it in the wrong
way. Perhaps it was the gentleness that had grated,
she thought. The other woman was most likely sick
of trite sympathy and of people who treated her like
a piece of cracked china.

And it was in a much sharper tone than any she
had used to Grant that Dorothy replied, 'Not as difficult as some. It would have been different, I dare
say, if I'd had a real talent, an urge to express myself,
but I can't pretend that I did. I was fairly competent,
but that's about the most anyone ever managed to say
for my work. In a way it was a relief to drop the whole
business.' She gave an awkward grimace. 'It gave me
a cast-iron excuse, the diagnosis. My grandfather was
a difficult man. I never could stand up to him. He'd
have been livid if I'd ever told him I was fed up with
trying to paint.'

Mandy didn't know how to reply to this. This
Dorothy Fernham wasn't anything like the comfortable soul she had seen in her daydreams; she had no
idea how to treat this real-life mother, and she wasn't

at all sure how she was going to be treated by her.
She had taken it for granted that her own artistic skills
would be welcomed and admired in this family, but
now it struck her that Dorothy might not respond like
that at all.

Incurable diseases don't turn people into saints, she
reminded herself; and lots of mothers and daughters
don't get on at all, even when they've known each
other all their lives. You didn't come expecting
miracles; you told yourself that often enough.

She stood up, and went to look at the pictures
hanging on the far wall. She saw as she approached
that most of them were small watercolours.

'Are any of these yours?'

'A couple. That sketch of the willow to your left
is mine, and the drawing of the cat below it.'

Mandy made out the pictures Dorothy had indicated. Her mother had been telling the truth, she saw
immediately. They were neatly drawn, well-composed,
but with no spark of inspiration, nothing about them
that held the eye. And they didn't hold hers for longer
than was polite, for there was something about the
central group of pictures, a half-dozen vibrant
watercolours of Broadland scenes, that seemed to have
been pulling her to them even from half-way across
the room.

'Your pictures are lovely, but these ones are absolutely wonderful!' she cried out.

'Aren't they?' Dorothy agreed. 'Those are Grandfather's, of course. Horace Blackwater. He was very
well known as a landscape painter.'

Grandfather's. Dorothy's grandfather, that was. He
would have been her own great-grandfather. And a

little more thought told her that he would also have been the great-grandfather of Frances's daughter. That was a happy coincidence: she would be able to acknowledge her precise relationship to him.

'How strange,' she said slowly, her eyes still on the pictures. 'I never knew before that I came from a family of painters.'

'Oh, yes. Most of the Blackwaters have painted, though none of the rest of us were as good as Horace. Of course, you might be, for all I know,' Dorothy added, a little tartly.

Mandy glanced back at her, apprehensively. 'My work's nothing like this,' she said hastily. 'I've been doing some watercolours of this kind of scene since I last came up to Norfolk, but the style I've been working on is quite different.'

'It would be. You'll find it harder now: harder to fix your own style, now you know how your great-grandfather saw it all.'

'Your great-grandfather?'

The sound of Grant's voice shook her, and she spun round automatically to locate the source of it. He was standing in the doorway. His eyes didn't avoid hers, as Dorothy's had; they connected instantly with her look, and fixed on it. But there was something cold in them now, not the fierce glow that had burned her earlier, and there was an odd accusing tone in his voice that stung even more fiercely, coming as it did right after Dorothy's painful taunt.

'That's right,' retorted Mandy. 'Dorothy and I were just working it out. Horace Blackwater was Frances's grandfather as well as her own, so he would have been my great-grandfather.'

'How interesting.'

Grant moved into the room as he spoke, and
Mandy's eyes followed him. His ordinary words had
been made more meaningful by the tone he had used:
he had sounded almost like a detective uncovering a
vital clue in a murder case. Why? Mandy wondered.
There was nothing odd in her response to the pictures, surely? Of course she was interested to see
Horace Blackwater's work. Surely any painter would
be, in the circumstances. Of course she admired the
pictures—but then, so would anybody with the faintest
sensitivity to fine works of art.

Dorothy rescued her, saying, 'There are hundreds
of Horace's paintings in the house. He lived here for
most of his life, and he painted Catwood Broad from
every possible angle. He didn't hang so many himself,
but my father put up a lot more after he died, and
I've just left them as I found them. There are hundreds
in drawers upstairs, too. There isn't the wallspace to
hang any more of them.'

Mandy half expected a sardonic comment to round
off this explanation, but it didn't come. Suddenly it
struck her that all Dorothy's earlier sharpness had
come after Grant had left the room. While he had
been listening she had been honey-sweet, as she was
now.

'I'd love to see them,' she said.

'You must, before you go.'

'Right now,' Grant said, 'it's time I was going. I
discovered that they've got a spare fanbelt in the
garage in Wroxham, and old Arthur has offered me
a lift in. I'll have to set off now, or I won't get there

before the garage shuts. I'll just show you your room, Mandy, and then I'll say goodbye.'

Dorothy tried to persuade him that he had time to drink a second glass of champagne first, but he politely and firmly refused. She didn't press him, but said, 'It's the blue room, Grant. And could you show Mandy the bathroom, and where to find the oil remover you used?'

'Of course.'

'And we'll see you on Sunday, for lunch?'

'Would I miss it?' Grant gave Dorothy a faint smile, and went over to kiss her lightly, before moving into the hall to pick up Mandy's bags once more.

Sunday lunch, Mandy thought to herself, as she followed him upstairs. Almost one of the family, Dorothy had said. He was clearly close to both Mr and Mrs Fernham, though it seemed equally clear now that he was no blood relation to either of them, but that the friendship had developed from his partnership with James Fernham in Catwood Wherrymen. From the way in which it had been said, she had the impression that his coming to Sunday lunch was a regular occurrence, and nothing to do with her own visit.

Was he married? she wondered. She hadn't noticed a wedding ring, and there had been no mention of a Mrs Livingstone, or any sign of a woman's presence in his car. And surely it wasn't usual for married men to regularly visit other people on their own for Sunday lunch, so presumably he wasn't. Not that it was any of her business what Grant Livingstone's domestic circumstances were, she firmly reminded herself.

'It's this room,' Grant said, shouldering open a heavy Victorian panelled door. He dropped her bags on the bed, and turned to face her as she entered.

She glanced around the room, and couldn't help exclaiming with pleasure. It was one of the prettiest bedrooms she had ever seen. The walls were Wedgwood blue, hung with still more watercolours of the Broads, and a lace bed-covering and a pile of lacy trimmed cushions on the pair of low cane chairs added a feminine touch.

She wasn't so absorbed in it, though, that she failed to catch the edge of Grant's sudden smile, and she turned to share her own pleasure more openly with him.

'Heron's Nest is one of those houses that's much more attractive inside than out.'

Her eyes widened a little: it wasn't the kind of comment she had expected from him. 'You're right,' she agreed.

'It had a second-rate architect, but generations of talented people have lived here.'

Mandy smiled again, broadly this time. 'My family,' she said, with a sudden rush of emotion.

Their eyes met once more, not with surprise or shock, but in a shared warmth of thought and feeling. But then, quite suddenly, it was as if a shutter had been drawn over Grant's face. His brows lowered, his eyes narrowed, and there was real coldness in his voice as he said tersely, 'So you say.'

'So I say? But, Grant, you can't doubt that!'

He did, that was obvious. He held her gaze for a moment, and then he said, in a low voice that had a dangerous edge to it, 'Why didn't you tell James that you were Frances Blackwater's daughter?'

Mandy pretended to be puzzled, though in fact the question didn't surprise her; she had guessed that it was coming.

'Tell him? But that's no secret, James and Dorothy know I'm Frances's daughter.'

'In the office,' Grant persisted. 'In the office at the yard, James told you how much you looked like Frances. And you said you were related, but you didn't say then that you were her daughter.'

'Oh, then!' She gave a low giggle that she hoped sounded convincingly like relief. 'No, you're right, I didn't tell him then.'

'Why not?'

'You'll think this really silly.'

She hoped that he would say something reassuring, but he didn't. He just waited, silent and menacing, for her explanation. Mandy stumbled determinedly on. 'You see, Frances is such a common name in the Blackwater family. I've come across at least a dozen Frances Blackwaters since I've been drawing up my family tree. Several of them are more or less the same age, all born around the 1940s and 50s, and my mother's just one of them. When James mentioned the name Frances, I thought there was a good chance that he meant my mother, but I honestly wasn't sure. So I thought it would be better not to say anything until I'd had a chance to talk to Dorothy, and see if I was right.'

'You weren't sure that Frances Blackwater was your mother?' Grant repeated incredulously.

'*A* Frances Blackwater was, but I wasn't sure that it was the Frances Blackwater who had lived in Norfolk. You see, Grant, my mother died when I was a baby, and I've only ever seen one blurred photograph of her. My grandparents are dead too, and I never knew any of my Blackwater relations at all. That's why it means so much to me now to meet Dorothy and James, and to find a whole new family.'

The knowledge that this at least was true gave her words real conviction, she hoped, but she was conscious that she hadn't completely allayed Grant's suspicions. He stared at her, as if he was thinking that the tale she was telling was too unlikely to be a complete invention; but equally, too unlikely to be the whole truth either.

'Grant,' she went on, sensing that he was poised on an edge of uncertainty and might yet be tipped either way, 'why on earth should I lie about this? I don't understand why you're acting as if you're suspicious of me. Why would I want to come to Heron's Nest, why would I want to meet Dorothy and James, if I wasn't really a relative of theirs?'

'Oh, for heaven's sake! You must see——'

'See what?' Mandy persisted.

But it was too late; he had decided now not to tell her what she must see. He turned away from her, abruptly, and paced the short distance to the window. He stared out of it for a moment, as if the grey expanse of Catwood Broad would swallow his answer. Then he looked back, and said curtly, 'Don't try to nose around this house. I know Dorothy can't get upstairs to check on you, but I'll be checking, you can be sure.'

'Nose around?' echoed Mandy, her voice rising fast. 'Nose around? I don't nose around other people's houses, I'll have you know!'

'I hope you're right,' Grant replied, brutally ignoring her anger. He crossed the room and pushed past her, and disappeared through the doorway. He reappeared briefly to add, 'The bathroom's the second door on the left, down the corridor,' and then he was gone.

Mandy stared at the empty doorway after he had disappeared. Nose around? What on earth had he meant? He had caught her once, sitting innocently on the lawn of Heron's Nest—not *nosing around* the terrace or the potting sheds, but simply sitting on the lawn with her drawing-board—and ever since he had been treating her like a criminal. Why? If the Fernhams had been stinking rich she might have thought he was taking her for a con-woman, but this was no millionaire's pad, simply an ordinary, pleasant country house. She couldn't believe that there was anything to steal here that would be worth the trouble of such a masquerade. Anyway, her family resemblance to the Blackwaters was striking, as James had made clear: didn't that confirm at least the gist of her story?

It was a mystery, but one that she wasn't going to solve by staring at an empty doorway, especially while her mother was waiting downstairs for her to reappear. She followed Grant's directions to the bathroom, and was relieved to find that he had left a tub of grease-solvent by the basin.

By the time that she had freshened up after her journey, changed her blouse—which had several per-

sistent oil stains, she had discovered to her regret—
and scrubbed the last traces of grease from her hands
and arms, she knew from the noises downstairs that
James Fernham had returned. It was a relief to her.
At least James wasn't hostile and suspicious, and with
him there she would be saved from the ordeal of
another one-to-one talk with Dorothy until she had
had a chance to get to know her mother a little better.

She cast a quick glance in the mirror. She had re-
placed the white silk blouse with a dove-grey cotton
top, an old but favourite garment that went well with
her blue skirt and grey eyes. She looked perfectly
suitable, she thought: not impressive, perhaps, but she
wasn't trying to impress the Fernhams in that kind of
way. Rich relatives, indeed, she thought mockingly,
as she made her way downstairs. It was a laughable
idea that she might be here to steal from the Fernhams.
It took more than one bottle of champagne to make
a rich relative!

The Fernhams were still in the living-room, and
James—giving the lie to Dorothy's earlier remark—
was just opening a second bottle of champagne. He
came over to Mandy with a glassful and she accepted
it gratefully.

She found over dinner that her first impressions of
James hadn't been mistaken; he seemed a charming,
easy-going man, devoted to his invalid wife, and absorbed in his boatbuilding and hire business. Dorothy
too was more relaxed in her husband's company than
she had been earlier, and, though there were a few
uneasy moments for Mandy, she genuinely enjoyed
the evening with the two of them.

Grant might have suspected her story about Frances Blackwater, she thought, but James seemed to have no such doubts. Nor did he show any great interest in the ins and outs of the Blackwater family relationships: the subject was only mentioned once in passing.

Mandy told both him and Dorothy a little about her life in London, and explained how she was slowly gaining a reputation—and work—as an artist and illustrator, and how she managed to make ends meet with the occasional stint as a temporary clerk or typist.

'You must have left home young,' Dorothy said thoughtfully.

'Just after my eighteenth birthday. I suppose that is quite young,' agreed Mandy. She glanced anxiously at Dorothy—she didn't want to give her mother the impression that her adoption had been a disaster, and add to whatever guilt she might already be feeling. 'Mind, I'm on good terms with my parents,' she said with an awkward laugh. 'But they believed in giving me my independence as soon as I felt ready to strike out on my own, and in any case, their house is really too far out of town to make a good base for my kind of work.'

'We'll have to meet them too,' James said.

Oh, no! That wouldn't do at all. Mandy had never mentioned to the Masons her decision to search out her real mother, and she had no doubt that they would refuse to go along with her deception if they were to learn about it. 'They're not actually blood relations of yours,' she said cautiously.

'You think Mrs Mason might be a little...'

Mandy thought hard, through the slight haze that the champagne was bringing over her mind. Dorothy was right to prompt her: that was the line to take.

'She's been a wonderful stepmother,' she said with determined sincerity, 'but I think she might find it painful if I made a big song and dance about looking out my real mother's family.'

'Well, we'll leave you to guide us, Mandy,' James said. 'And there's no one else for us to meet? No half-sisters or brothers? No boyfriends?'

'James!' Dorothy protested. 'Mandy's far too young to have a serious boyfriend!'

Too young? Mandy thought, surprised. She was nineteen! OK, there wasn't anyone serious in her life, but she hadn't thought herself much too young for a boyfriend, it was just that the right one hadn't happened along yet. What an odd thing for Dorothy to say! Fortunately she was saved from thinking up a reply, because James said firmly, 'No, she's not, Dorothy. Don't forget, you were only twenty-one when we got married.'

'Twenty-one?' echoed Mandy.

'Straight out of art college, she was.' James smiled reminiscently. 'She wouldn't commit herself before she went away, and I almost had chickens thinking of all those young men she'd meet in London. So when she came back and I found out she was still fancy-free, I decided I wasn't going to waste any more time before I signed her up.'

Still fancy-free. How old was Dorothy now? Mandy couldn't help wondering. And how old had she been when she herself was born? Had it happened during those fancy-free years at art college? This wasn't the

time to pry, she knew, but she found it hard to rein
in her curiosity. She already knew that James Fernham
wasn't her natural father, and she couldn't help wondering how his courtship of Dorothy had tied in with
the affair that had led to her birth.

'But even if you did marry young, you must have
known each other a long time,' she prompted
cautiously.

'All our lives,' James agreed. 'Well, all Dorothy's
life, because I'm fourteen years older than Dorothy,
so I was no young boy myself when I tied the knot.
I came from Brown Common, Mandy, just a couple
of miles up the road. I always thought I'd like to marry
Dorothy Blackwater and come to live in Heron's Nest,
and that's what I did, and it suits me just as well as
I thought it would.' He turned to Dorothy, and gave
her a confident smile, as if he had never doubted that
it suited her just as perfectly.

Did it? Mandy wondered, remembering the secret
that Dorothy had never told him; remembering, too,
Dorothy's effusive manner with Grant. This was
something else that she couldn't possibly ask. Instead
she asked politely, 'So you bought the house right after
you were married?'

It was Dorothy who replied this time. 'Oh, no,' she
said, with sudden decisiveness. 'Didn't I tell you,
Mandy, that my grandfather had lived here? I inherited Heron's Nest when my father died, fifteen
years ago. This house is mine, and everything in it.'

CHAPTER FIVE

'WHAT would you like to do today, Mandy?' James Fernham asked over breakfast. 'It's a fine day: I could take you into Norwich, maybe, or to the coast?'

Mandy glanced nervously across the table at where Dorothy Fernham sat in her wheelchair. Though James wasn't a forceful man, she had noticed already that he was tending to take the lead in dealing with her, as if Dorothy, after taking the plunge and inviting her up to Heron's Nest, was now in some strange way fighting shy of her. From Dorothy's impassive expression, she had the impression that her mother really wouldn't mind if she and James went into Norwich together and left her alone all day.

But Mandy minded: she hadn't come to Heron's Nest so that she could go and sightsee in Norwich. She had come to get to know Dorothy, although she didn't want to make her mother feel that she was being pushed too far or too fast into an intimacy that might not come naturally to her.

'I'd really rather have a quiet day here,' she responded. 'There are several things I'd like to do. I'd like to take a better look at some of the paintings in the house, if you don't mind, and maybe do a little sketching myself.'

'Sketching? Right here, you mean, or would you rather go somewhere else?'

'Here would do fine, or maybe I'll just take a walk along the edge of the broad and hunt out an assortment of different angles to paint it from. The broad here is so beautiful, it would seem almost perverse to go anywhere else.'

'You must see some more of the other broads as well while you're here, though, Mandy,' Dorothy said. 'Perhaps James could take you out on the water tomorrow.'

'I'll certainly fix something up for you,' James agreed. 'But I'll leave you two together now, if you don't mind, and push off into Wroxham myself for a while.'

'OK, dear,' Dorothy said absently. 'You won't forget, will you, that it's the Tuddenhams' barbecue this evening?'

'Course not,' James assured her. 'You're invited too, Mandy. It might be a quiet do by your London standards, but I hope you'll enjoy it.'

'I'm sure I will,' she responded automatically. 'Now, can I just help with the breakfast things...'

'No need. Mrs Jackson does that. You go and see to your painting. Lunch will be around one o'clock, if that suits you.'

'Of course.' Mandy got up from the table, feeling strangely let down. Didn't Dorothy want to talk to her at all? she wondered unhappily. Didn't she want to look with her at Horace Blackwater's paintings, and tell her about the places he had painted and the things he had done? Apparently not. It looked as if she was expected to amuse herself, and to keep on treating Dorothy like the distant relation she was pretending to be, and not the mother that she really was.

But there was a whole week to go, she reminded herself, and no need for her and Dorothy to rush into confidences. She took a pad and pencil as she wandered around the house—thinking ruefully of Grant's ridiculous accusations about 'nosing'—and wrote down the names of some of the scenes that she found particularly attractive. Luckily, Horace Blackwater had made a habit of writing an inscription beneath each one of his watercolours.

Later that morning she took out a big map of the Norfolk Broads, and spent a pleasant hour trying to identify some of the locations, and to work out how she might perhaps get to some of them, so that she could see how much they had changed since her great-grandfather's day, and perhaps try painting them for herself. And in the afternoon she settled down on the edge of the lawn, not far from the spot she had chosen a fortnight before, and sketched happily, this time with no dark shadows or menacing accusations to disturb her tranquillity.

The drawings went well, but she couldn't help losing her concentration sometimes, glancing back towards the house and wondering where Dorothy was and what she was doing. Once Dorothy came out on to the terrace with Mrs Jackson, the daily help, for a few minutes, but otherwise there was no sign of her. Nor was there any sign of the owner of the dark shadow. Don't be ridiculous, she scolded herself: Grant doesn't live here, and there's absolutely no reason for him to come here on a Saturday afternoon.

She wondered, too, whether he would be coming to the Tuddenhams' barbecue, but from the way in which Dorothy had mentioned it she took it that there was no prospect of his escorting her there. Still, the faint possibility that he might be coming was enough to make her dress for the barbecue with special care. From what Dorothy had said she knew it would be a casual affair, but she wanted to wear a pretty dress, and she pulled out a simply cut summer frock in a pretty Liberty flowered print that was the most feminine garment in her small holiday wardrobe.

She washed her hair quickly, and rubbed it dry so that it stood out in a bright golden halo all around her head. She traced round her eyes two shades of grey shadow to bring out their deep colour, and finished her make-up by stroking on a light pink lipstick.

'We'll take Dorothy straight on to the terrace,' James Fernham told Valerie Tuddenham, as he, Dorothy and Mandy arrived at the Tuddenhams' house, which had proved to be only half a dozen houses distant from Heron's Nest. With the ease of much practice, he unfolded Dorothy's collapsible wheelchair, and Mandy helped him to lift Dorothy from the car into it. She followed behind as he pushed Dorothy through the house, and out on to a large flagged terrace overlooking the broad.

Valerie Tuddenham had followed them through, and Mandy was soon introduced to her and to some of the other guests. There were around twenty people on the terrace and lawns, many of them clustering around the barbecue fire which Mike Tuddenham was building up to a steady glow. Out on the broad, the laughter that came from a couple of rowing-boats showed that the party was extending there as well.

'You go down to the shore, Mandy,' Dorothy said. 'I'll stay here and talk to Mrs Tuddenham.'

Another brush-off, Mandy thought unhappily, though she knew that the barbecue wasn't the occasion for a serious talk with Dorothy. But there was something else: a touch of barely veiled bitterness in her mother's voice that made her sense that Dorothy wished it were she who could run down to the broad and hunt out the people who were so obviously having the most fun. She glanced at Mrs Tuddenham, Valerie's elderly mother, who was also wheelchair-bound, and decided that she would only make things worse if she didn't do as Dorothy suggested.

The Tuddenhams' garden was even larger than the garden at Heron's Nest, and it took her several minutes to cross the smooth expanse of lawn. She saw when she was perhaps fifty paces away from the shore that Grant was in one of the rowing-boats.

Mandy stopped a moment, and watched him. There were a lot of people milling about the garden, and she was confident that he hadn't seen her yet.

He wasn't alone. In the boat with him were two women, one a slim, dark-haired girl, and another with curly brown hair and glasses, and a round-faced, rather plump man. The dark-haired girl was sitting next to Grant on the middle bench, and they appeared to be arguing over who would take the oars. The girl leaned right over in front of Grant, and grabbed at the oar he was holding. She pushed it right out of his hand and into the water, and Mandy saw him throw back his head and laugh loudly.

An uncomfortable little spasm sneaked through her insides, and she turned away hurriedly. There wasn't room for her in the boat, that was obvious; she'd do better to go and join the crowd around the barbecue fire.

'Mandy!'

Grant's loud, rather harsh voice carried easily to her, and she turned back to him with uncalculated eagerness.

'Mandy!' he shouted again. 'Come and join us!'

She went a little closer to the shore.

'There really isn't enough space for anyone else, Grant,' she heard the dark-haired girl say, in a pettish voice.

'Of course there is, if you move into the bows, Pam.'

Pam glowered at Mandy; Mandy glowered back.

'Watch it, Grant, we're drifting away from your oar,' the other man said.

Grant transferred his attention to the floating oar. He didn't really want her in the boat, Mandy thought suddenly: he was only being polite. He had obviously come to the barbecue with the girl called Pam, and Pam just as obviously wasn't keen to share his attentions with Mandy. If she persisted she would only embarrass and annoy him. She murmured a few words, though she knew he wasn't listening, and walked away quickly.

She had a good time for the rest of the evening, but she deliberately kept her distance from Grant, even after he came ashore, and he made no move to approach her at all.

'Fine day for your trip, Mandy,' James said brightly the next morning.

'Looks perfect,' she agreed. 'Where are we going?'

'Actually, I hope you don't mind, but I won't be coming with you. I've had a busy week at the yard and hardly seen Dorothy at all, so I thought I'd grab the chance to spend a quiet day with her while you go off searching out the best spots for sketching.'

You've hardly seen Dorothy? Mandy thought with annoyance. I've seen even less of her! She pushed down the rapidly surfacing self-pity, plastered on a bright smile, and said, 'Of course I don't mind. That is, if you'll trust a learner driver like me with one of your boats!'

'I would,' James grinned, 'but I doubt if Grant would! This isn't what I had in mind at all, though, Mandy. We wouldn't want to leave our visitor all alone. No, Grant offered last night to take you out himself in our little runabout, the *Pink Pussycat*. He's usually over here for Sunday lunch, but this week it'll be a hamper for the two of you. He knows the Broads just as well as I do, and he says he'll be happy to take you to wherever you want to go.'

Mandy's stomach seemed to have done a sudden dip to somewhere below her knees. A day out on the Broads with Grant! It was the last thing she had expected—and just about the last thing she wanted, after the antagonism he had shown to her earlier. But if he really had offered to take her, then it seemed that she had no choice but to gratefully accept the suggestion.

'That's very kind of him,' she managed to say.

'I said I'd drop you off at the yard, and he'll meet you there. The boat's there, of course, and it's a better spot to start from. Tennish, we said, so we'll set off in my car as soon as you're ready.'

It was almost nine-thirty then, so Mandy had barely enough time to gather together her drawing things. James pulled up his Volvo in the forecourt of Catwood Wherrymen at a few minutes past ten, and she saw immediately that Grant's Range Rover was already parked there.

The *Pink Pussycat* was a small motor cruiser, James had explained, that he and Grant kept for running around the Broads. Grant had moved her from her regular berth and tied her up on the riverbank, and he was waiting on board as Mandy and James came down the towpath, carrying the hamper between them.

'What time do you plan to get back, Grant?' James asked, when they had stowed the hamper and Mandy's drawing things in the tiny covered cabin.

'Oh, don't worry about us,' Grant said. 'I'll give Mandy a lift back to Heron's Nest myself. So long as I get her there by seven, say...'

'Six-thirty, if she wants any supper.' James laughed, and waved a hand as he turned to walk back to the car park. 'Have a good day, both of you.'

She turned to watch him for a moment, until he disappeared behind the boatsheds.

'Coming on board?' Grant asked, with a hint of sarcasm.

'Yes, of course.'

She had to take his helping hand to step safely on to the little boat, and even after he had released her there didn't seem to be anywhere where she could get more than a couple of feet away from him. It was such a small boat, and Grant was such a large man. He had the grace and economy of movement of a man who spent much of his life on boats, but Mandy felt clumsy by comparison, and she didn't know how to keep out of his way.

'Sit there for now,' he said, sensing her confusion, 'and I'll get her going. Then later you can take a turn at the wheel if you want to.'

'I really don't mind much.'

'Then you can do just as I say.' He gave her a sudden bright smile. 'Anywhere special you want to go?'

'I had a few ideas, but you probably have better ones.'

'I dare say I know the rivers round here better than you do,' he calmly agreed. 'I thought we'd set off down the Bure—this is the Bure, of course: it's the river that runs through Wroxham and north-west to Aylsham—with maybe a quick detour into Hoveton Little Broad, and go down as far as Ranworth. There's a dike that leads off the Bure towards Ranworth Broad and Ranworth village. Ranworth Broad's closed to vessels, but there's a nature trail through the marshes and a conservation centre overlooking the water, where you can look out for many of the Broadland birds. We can tie up at the wharf there for lunch.'

'Sounds fine,' she agreed nervously.

'OK, let's go.'

After they had cast off, there was nothing for Mandy to do but watch as Grant set a tidy course through the maze of boats that threaded across the Bure, in the direction of Hoveton Little Broad. Steering the *Pink Pussycat* didn't demand anything like the kind of skill that a sailing-boat like the *Grey Lady* required, she knew, but all the same she enjoyed watching Grant's easy efficiency.

'Go and sun yourself if you want to,' he suggested after a few minutes.

'Where?' she asked dubiously. There didn't seem to be any expanse of decking remotely large enough for her to stretch out on.

'On the cabin roof. It's quite safe, I won't be going fast.'

'In a minute.'

'Did you bring some tanning lotion? You want to watch the sun. It feels quite cool while we're moving, but it'll be strong enough by now to burn you in no time.'

'There's some in my bag.'

'If you take the wheel when you've found it, I'll rub it in for you.'

Self-consciously, she peeled off her T-shirt and shorts to reveal a pink and white striped bikini that now felt much briefer that it had seemed when she had bought it the year before. She rummaged in her bag, and brought the bottle of suntan oil over to Grant.

'Just keep going straight. I'll take over if there are any problems.'

Mandy tried to concentrate on the quiet river ahead and on keeping the boat moving parallel with the wooded banks, and not on Grant's cool fingers tracing circles on the skin of her bare back and shoulders as he rubbed in the oil, but it wasn't easy: the sensuousness of his touch made all sorts of unruly thoughts creep into her mind. She was rather sorry when he lifted his hands, and said in a gruff voice, 'That should do it.'

'Thanks.'

'You could do the same for me, before you move back to the roof. Just on my shoulders, the rest of me never burns.'

She kept her eyes on the river, but she could hear him stripping off the blue shirt he had been wearing, and she cast a sideways glance at him as he set two firm hands on her sides, and planted her a step sideways so that he could regain the wheel. He had a firm, muscular chest, with a thick thatch of reddish-brown hair curling across it.

She moved behind him, standing very close in the confined space, and dribbled a little of the oil on to his bare shoulders. She felt him flinch a little at the coolness of it, and then she brought her fingers to work, smoothing it into his skin. It was firm and re-silient to the touch, and she could feel the muscles move beneath the surface as he twisted the cruiser's wheel.

'Thank you,' Grant said, with a touch of amusement a few minutes later, and Mandy realised to her embarrassment that she had been letting her hands linger on his shoulders, long after all trace of the suntan oil had been rubbed in. She retreated hurriedly to the cabin roof, stretched out on her front, and propped her face on her hands, watching the Broadland scenery as they chugged along the river. The sun was quite high by then, and the varnished wood felt hot and smooth beneath her.

They wove into and out of Hoveton Little Broad, a small broad that was deep enough for navigation only in the centre, Grant told her, and carried on through the little town of Horning. Then came a quiet rural stretch of river, until at last Grant called out, 'That's Ranworth, over there. See the church tower?'

Mandy stirred. She had been half asleep, lulled by the purring of the boat's engine and the warmth of the sun. She reached out a hand to feel her back, and decided that it was probably rather more than well-baked by now, so she slipped off the roof and back into the cabin to join Grant.

'It looks quite a way away,' she said.

'Maybe a mile and a half. We'll do about a mile of that by water, and walk the last half-mile up to the church.'

'We don't want to go into the church, do we?' Mandy half-protested.

'Of course we do. It has the finest rood screen in Norfolk, fifteenth century. And from the top of the tower you get a wonderful view across the Broads.'

She glanced at him in surprise. He didn't seem like an artistic man, but he was, she thought to herself. He had shown his awareness of fine things in her room at Heron's Nest, and now he was making it clear again. It wasn't just that he had a deep knowledge of the Broads and the surrounding countryside, he also had a good sense of judgement. If he said the rood screen and the view were wonderful, then she could well believe that they were.

Grant moored at a small wooden quay next to the chain which separated the forbidden waters of Ranworth Broad from the navigable cut, and led Mandy along the bank to the conservation centre. A neat wooden building, it was built out into the broad itself on stilts, and had windows all round, set with binoculars from which visitors could spy out the coots, plovers and herons of the broadland. Along the edge of the broad, Grant pointed out the humped backs of sunken wherries, all of them clearly long beyond restoration.

From the centre there was a planked walk through the different varieties of semi-marshland that surrounded the Broads proper, which emerged near Ranworth village and the church. The planks weren't slippery, but the walk was narrow, and it seemed natural for Grant to take Mandy's hand when they had to pause to let some other tourists pass them. He kept it firmly wrapped in his large hand as they walked up the road to the church.

The rood screen, with its twelve brooding medieval saints, was as beautiful as he had promised. Mandy would happily have lingered in the church taking in every small detail while Grant did the climb up the tower alone, but Grant insisted that she must come up with him, and eventually he almost dragged her towards the narrow door, and nudged her ahead of him up a lengthy spiral staircase.

They emerged into a bell-loft, with heavy wooden beams giving them tantalising glimpses of a peal of old bells, and a rickety-looking stepladder that led still further upwards.

'Fascinating,' she murmured. 'But this is as far as I go, Grant.'

'As far as you go? You can't see anything from here!'

'To be honest, I don't *want* to see anything. Perhaps I should have warned you earlier, but I've always suffered from vertigo.'

'Nonsense. There's a parapet, and I'll hold on to you.' He grabbed her hand again, and urged her towards the ladder.

'You go first,' she pleaded.

'If you promise to follow me.'

He clambered up the steep ladder with surprising agility, and then reached down to take Mandy's hand and help her after him. There was one more ladder to negotiate, and then they emerged on to a steeply sloping roof.

'Sit down,' Grant commanded.

She really hadn't any choice, as he drew her down next to him on to the warm lead roofing, and wrapped his arm around her.

'Now look.'

She looked. It was a wonderful view. The countryside was flat, and they could see for miles across broads, rivers, woods and marshes. Grant kept holding her close as he pointed out to her the route they had taken, and told her the names of some of the villages they could see.

Mandy had always hated looking down on things from a great height, but it wasn't possible to be scared, somehow, when she could feel the warmth of Grant's strong body through his thin shirt, and the light but firm grip of his hand on her upper arm. They sat there for some time, gazing out at the scenery, until a commotion just below told them that some more people were coming up the ladder, and Grant slowly got to his feet.

'That's your education for today. Come on, let's go down and find our lunch.'

Going down the narrow, juddering ladders felt even worse than climbing up them, but Grant seemed to sympathise with her nervousness, and Mandy wasn't so self-conscious now about grabbing on to him when she felt unsteady. They walked side by side in pleasant contentment back down the lane, and across the nature trail towards the quay.

Mrs Jackson had packed them a treat of a picnic lunch: cold chicken legs roasted with herbs, crisp brown rolls, a pot of creamy coleslaw and a large hunk of Brie, washed down with a bottle of white wine. She had wrapped the wine in wet newspaper, and it was still quite cool, despite the warmth of the day. Mandy devoured a good half of everything and sat back with a sigh of pleasure.

'This is the life!'

'Says a good working girl,' Grant teased. 'I haven't seen you get out your sketchpad once.'

'How could I when we were moving all the time?' she protested. 'But I would like to do a sketch from here, if you don't mind us staying for a while.'

'Not at all. Are you sure this is the place you want? There are dozens of other places where I can tie up, if you'd prefer a different view.'

'This will do fine.' The view from the public jetty would be a familiar one to many people, she knew, but that made it no less attractive to her.

'Wake me when you're ready to move on, then.' Grant uncurled his long legs, unfastened his shirt and threw it on to the bench, and clambered up on to the cabin roof. He stretched out, and gave every indication of going to sleep in the sunshine.

She gave him a surreptitious glance or two as she got out her sketching things. His long body stretched almost from end to end of the cabin, and the sun struck highlights off his reddish-brown hair. There was an animal strength and magnetism about him. And he could be such good company, she thought, when he wasn't throwing vague accusations at her all the time. But she couldn't help remembering Pam's possessive gestures the evening before, and she knew that, though he hadn't altogether hidden his attraction to her, he had given her no indication that he wanted to act on it.

Anyway, how could he? She was only in Norfolk for a week, and then she would be leaving Grant and the Fernhams behind, and going back to her own life in London.

She walked a few yards along the riverside path, and found a spot where a wooden bench had been set by the pathway, just out of sight of the *Pink Pussycat*, to set up her easel.

Once she had started, she soon became absorbed in the technical problems of sketching the scenery. It wasn't easy, she already appreciated, to capture the quiet perfection without making it look flat and rather boring on paper. Again, she felt that she would get the best results by making notes for watercolours that brought out the subtle colour contrasts of the marshland vegetation and the still water.

A few people passed by on the path, going to and from the conservation centre, and some of them stopped to glance at her work, but Mandy was used to being watched as she drew, and she paid little attention to them. She began to sketch increasingly rapidly, pulling page after page from her pad in her eagerness to prepare the groundwork for a long painting session once she got back to London.

She had completely forgotten about Grant, and it was a genuine surprise to her when she gave a quick glance at a passer-by who was peering over her shoulder, and realised on a second glance that it was him. He grinned back at her.

'You don't mind being watched while you're at work, do you?'

She didn't mind, exactly—she was rather pleased that he had finally shown an interest in what she was doing—but he *had* unnerved her. He was unnerving her still, standing so close and bending over her.

'Not as a rule. You just took me by surprise.'

'I'd been watching you from a distance for a few minutes, but you seemed so absorbed, I decided I'd have to come closer to get your attention.'

'Well, you've got it,' she said unnecessarily. 'Did you want to move on now?'

'There's no hurry.' He slid down on to the bench, just next to her. 'It's a little after four. We ought to start getting back in the next half-hour, if you want to be in time for supper. But take as long as you need.'

'I've just about finished,' she replied. 'I just wanted to do one more sketch...'

'Shall I wait, or would you rather I went back to the boat?'

Mandy hesitated. She liked having Grant sit next to her, but at the same time she was conscious that she wouldn't be able to concentrate on her sketching while he was there. 'Go back, please,' she said.

He went. She ripped the top sheet off her drawing-pad, and started on the last sketch. But it was no good, her concentration and her inspiration both seemed to have left her. She persevered for ten minutes, partly for appearances' sake, then packed up her things and made her way back along the path.

Grant was sitting on the roof of the *Pink Pussycat*. He watched her approach, then came down to help her on board.

'Can I see what you did?' he asked, as she set down her sketchpad.

'If you like.' Mandy sat down on the bench in the cabin, and handed him the pad.

He leafed slowly through the sketches she had done that afternoon. There were a couple of dozen of them, some quite detailed, but many no more than roughs with scrawled notes on them. He stopped to look at several more closely.

'You're reckoning to do watercolours from these?' he asked, finally looking up at her.

'That's right. Obviously these aren't for use as they are, they're just working sketches to guide me when I paint. I know they're not particularly wonderful as works of art.'

'They're good of their kind, I think,' Grant said seriously. 'You obviously know what you want to achieve, and you set about it very professionally.'

'I *am* a professional,' she retorted. 'It's not just a hobby—I do try to make my living by painting and drawing.'

'Sure, I know.' He met her eyes, fixing her gaze and holding it. He knew exactly what that look did to her, she thought. Did it do the same to him? She had assumed it must until then, but suddenly she wasn't sure what he meant the look to communicate. There was the intense attraction she had sensed earlier, but at the same time there seemed to be something else: a wariness, almost a hint of his former suspicion once more.

'I should have listened to your plans,' he said thoughtfully. 'I'm sorry. I'd planned out the day as a sort of holiday, but really you meant it to be a working day, didn't you? And I haven't given you much choice of scenes to sketch, or let you direct me to where you wanted to go.'

'Not at all,' she said awkwardly. 'I've got a lot done this afternoon. And I've really enjoyed it.'

'So have I.' That level gaze, from those curiously arresting eyes, held hers for just a moment longer; then very slowly Grant's face moved closer to hers.

She only realised that he was intending to kiss her in the split second before his lips touched hers. It was too late to move or to react, too late to do anything but wait for the first gentle pressure of his mouth. It felt warm, sun-warmed. Grant's arms moved round her, and he drew her closer into his embrace.

Her lips parted, under the steadily increasing pressure of his, and she felt his tongue move softly around their inner surfaces, caressing, teasing, before nudging its way into her mouth. It barely sought out her own, then withdrew, leaving just a hint of un-fulfilled erotic promise behind it.

He moved away from her rapidly, almost abruptly, as if he had suddenly thought better of making love to her. He stood, and picked up the sketchpad, stowing it away under the cabin bench in a businesslike manner. Mandy watched him. Her whole body seemed to have lost a skin: every nerve-ending seemed to be on fire, and she could still sense every place where he had touched her.

Grant straightened, as far as he could in the low cabin. 'OK with you if I take the wheel again?'

'Yes, fine,' she answered automatically. She couldn't think straight. The kiss had affected her far too much, she thought, annoyed with herself. It was only a quick kiss, for heaven's sake, and here she was mooning about like a lovesick sixteen-year-old! 'I'll go and grab a bit more sun before it goes down,' she added, and quickly made her way out of the cabin.

CHAPTER SIX

MONDAY and Tuesday were both cloudier days, and on Tuesday, at Dorothy's suggestion, Mandy accepted a lift from James to Wroxham station and took the train into Norwich.

She was feeling a little low. Heron's Nest was just as pleasant a place to stay as she had expected, and Dorothy and James had both been very kind to her, but that was all it was—kindness, no more. Dorothy seemed now to have settled into a sort of distant friendliness. Everything about her manner warned Mandy off asking intimate questions, and she had begun to think that she would leave Norfolk knowing no more than she had known when she had arrived.

Grant hadn't contacted her again either, or reappeared at the house, and she couldn't help feeling disappointed at that too. It was as if things hadn't yet reached an even keel in her relationship with him; she couldn't help feeling that there was a great deal of unfulfilled potential in it. But he didn't seem to want to take things any further, and she was conscious that she wasn't in any position to press him.

She went to Norwich with no plans, except to look around the city, of which she knew very little; to see the cathedral, perhaps, and the castle, and some of the shops. Dorothy rarely went into Norwich, she had told Mandy, and had given her little advice on where to go or what to see.

The cathedral was beautiful, set in quiet closes of old houses, with a green expanse of playing-fields sweeping down to the river. Mandy spent most of the morning there, looking around and making a few quick sketches, and then, exhausted, hunted out a small café where she could buy a cheap lunch.

The café owner suggested that she make her way back to the town centre via Elm Hill, a pretty cobbled street, and Mandy happily accepted his advice. She was barely half-way up the steep, twisting street when she passed a small art gallery, and stopped, drawn by a picture that was displayed in the window.

She pushed her face to the window to look at it more closely, and immediately realised what had caught her eye. The picture was a watercolour of a Broadland scene, and from the style and the colouring Mandy was immediately sure that it was by Horace Blackwater.

Without another thought, she pushed open the door to the little gallery.

The woman sitting at the far end, reading a paperback, looked up as the door jangled.

'Can I help you?' she asked—a little sniffily, taking in Mandy's rather battered jeans, yellow cotton top, and the gay striped scarf she was using as a makeshift belt.

'Perhaps.' Mandy's first thought had been no more than to come in and look more closely at the picture, but now she was beginning to think that it would be nice to buy it. She really liked the idea of owning a Horace Blackwater of her own, and she wouldn't have dreamed of manoeuvring Dorothy into giving her one.

'Could I take a look at the painting in the window?
The watercolour?'

The gallery assistant reluctantly left her chair, and
crossed to the window. 'It's a Horace Blackwater,'
she said, as she reached for the picture. 'Of Alderfen
Broad, one of the less well-known broads.' She
glanced at it, with a sympathetic, appraising look
which warmed Mandy a little towards her.

Mandy took another look too. She didn't recognise
the view, but the painting itself was just as she had
thought it to be at first glance: a classic example of
her great-grandfather's work, bright without being
gaudy, delicately drawn. She wanted it.

'It's lovely,' she breathed.

'It's quite a nice example,' the woman conceded.
'I've got another couple of Blackwaters in the drawers,
but this is the only one I have ready-framed.'

'I didn't particularly want a frame . . .' Mandy murmured. It had struck her that it might be embarrassing to return to Heron's Nest with a framed
example of Horace Blackwater's art; she wanted it to
be unobtrusive. And buying a watercolour ready
framed tended to add quite a bit to the price, she knew.

'Let me look out the others, then,' the woman said.
She went to a big draughtsman's cabinet at the back
of the gallery, and peered at the labels on the drawers.
After a few moments' rustling through tissue paper,
she came up with two small, unframed watercolours.
They were neither of them quite as perfect as the
picture of Alderfen Broad, but they were both good
of their kind, and Mandy found that she recognised
the view in the smaller one. It was Ranworth Broad,

sketched from almost the position she had taken herself two days before.

'That one,' she said decisively.

'You're sure?'

'Quite sure.'

'You wouldn't like to take the two? They'd make a very striking pair, hung close together.'

'I don't think I could afford that,' replied Mandy honestly. 'Though you haven't told me the price yet,' she added.

'I haven't fixed a firm price for it. Let me see. Unframed, as you see it—shall we say, two hundred and fifty pounds?'

'Two hundred and fifty pounds!'

The woman's eyes narrowed. 'There's a great deal of demand for Blackwaters these days,' she said stiffly. 'Though this one is quite small. I think I might be able to allow you a discount, and accept two hundred and twenty for it. Cash, of course.'

Two hundred and twenty pounds cash? That was more than Mandy's current account held, more than she spent on artists' materials in a year. However much she coveted the little watercolour, she knew she couldn't possibly pay such a sum for it.

'I'm sorry,' she said regretfully. 'I'm afraid I've wasted your time.'

'I really don't think I can go any lower,' the assistant said.

It wouldn't have been any use to bargain. The picture cost at least five times as much as Mandy had estimated. She repeated her apology, and hurriedly backed out of the gallery.

There was a wooden seat, fastened round a big tree, at the top of Elm Hill, and she subsided on to this a moment later. Two hundred and fifty pounds for a small watercolour by Horace Blackwater! She had had no idea that her great-grandfather's work was in such demand.

After a short rest she walked on, and when she came to another small gallery she almost rushed past it. But in this gallery the paintings in the window were clearly, and moderately, priced, and after a moment's hesitation Mandy went in to browse.

'I'm not buying,' she said, when the elderly owner wandered over. 'Just admiring, I'm afraid.'

'That's all right, my dear. I'm happy to have people linger, it encourages other people to follow them in. What's your own preference? These abstracts over here, perhaps?'

The man was so friendly that Mandy soon found herself pouring out her tale. He nodded sympathetically as she finished it. 'I'm afraid she's right, my dear,' he said. 'There's a well-nigh inexhaustible demand for really good oils and watercolours of Norfolk scenery, and Horace Blackwater's reputation has grown massively over the past few years. He's one for the American tourists these days.'

'That's hard on the English tourists,' she said regretfully.

'Oh, I try to cater for them too. I sell a lot of this kind of thing. Much more moderately priced, but still good of its kind.' He pointed to a group of more modern watercolours of local views.

Mandy crossed to inspect them. 'These are very much like my own work,' she said.

'Are they, my dear? You're an amateur painter yourself, then?'

'No, a professional.' Mandy explained about the mix of work she had been doing, and about the views of Catwood Broad that Walt had been selling for her.

'I'd like to see some of them,' the gallery owner said. 'They won't fetch quite the price here that they would in London, but pretty watercolours do move quite quickly, and if yours really are up to the right standard, I might well be interested in taking a steady supply from you.'

'Would you really?' she exclaimed. 'I haven't any watercolours with me, I'm afraid, but I've some sketches of the cathedral that I did this morning, and I could call in again with some finished examples of my work.'

'Let's see the sketches.'

She left the gallery a few minutes later, after giving the man her name and address and collecting his card, with a new spring in her step. He had liked her sketches, and after seeing them he had been even more eager to see some examples of her watercolours.

It was always hard to find the right outlet for her work, but that little gallery would be ideal, she thought. It wasn't until she was back at the station that she came down to earth, and realised that she wouldn't be able to supply a Norwich dealer with regular Broadland scenes when she was returning to London very soon. But the offer had encouraged and cheered her, and it was still on her mind when she got back to Heron's Nest.

To her surprise, Grant was there—for practical reasons. He had come to go over some papers with

James after supper, he said, but even so he greeted her with a warmth that buoyed her mood still further.

Over supper Dorothy asked what she had done in Norwich, and, though she was careful not to mention the Blackwater, she did tell them about the second gallery.

Grant nodded. 'It's true,' he said. 'You do have a good eye, and anyone who knows the business would see from your sketches that your paintings are worth a look, too. Mind, I think you'd do better to sell them in London.'

'Pricewise, perhaps,' Mandy agreed. 'But my watercolours are the sort of thing that appeals to tourists, and the Norfolk scenes might well sell faster here. The man wanted a regular supply, though, and I'm just not in a position to provide him with one, so it's really not a practicable proposition.'

'And what will you be doing in London instead?' James asked. 'Turning out views of Piccadilly Circus and Trafalgar Square?'

Mandy gave a wry smile. 'Hardly. My technique isn't suited to that. I'll probably be back at my temping for the next few weeks. It's the start of the holiday season, so there's lots of temporary typing work available at the moment.'

'That's terrible!' Dorothy exclaimed. 'How *can* you go back to clerical work when you could be painting? And selling your paintings, too?'

'I really don't have any choice, Dorothy,' she answered quietly. 'I have to be self-supporting, and at the moment that means alternating between painting and typing.'

James said, 'But there's a very obvious choice, my dear. You must spend the summer here, at Heron's Nest.'

Mandy stared at him. 'No, I couldn't possibly,' she said.

'But you must!' Dorothy broke in. 'You're right, James, it's the perfect answer. It would be no trouble at all to have you here, and it would give you a chance to really get on with your painting. You wouldn't find it hard to pay your way, surely, if you managed to sell watercolours through a Norwich gallery and a London gallery? And there are plenty of other outlets around the county. There are galleries in Wells and Cromer and Yarmouth, even in Wroxham. I have plenty of contacts, because I've always dealt with my grandfather's work, so I could introduce you to the gallery owners. I'm sure you would sell just about every watercolour you managed to produce.'

Dorothy sounded as lively and enthusiastic as Mandy had known her, and it touched her to hear the eagerness in Dorothy's voice. True, Dorothy always seemed to make a special effort when Grant was around, but, even so, Mandy reckoned the enthusiasm was genuine. It was the first sign of real warmth Dorothy had shown towards her since their first phone call—and over her painting, too, which she had sensed from the start would be a sore point with her less talented mother. Admittedly James had been the first to make the suggestion, but even so it was really generous of Dorothy to second it so eagerly.

She didn't want to say no out of hand; that would be a poor reward for the effort Dorothy was making. And it *was* a tempting offer. She could see that it

would work. She wouldn't be in anyone's way at
Heron's Nest, and she would be able to produce pretty,
saleable watercolours of the Broadland very quickly—
maybe even several a day. They wouldn't be works of
genius to rival Horace Blackwater's, but it would be
enjoyable painting them, and she would almost certainly make more money than she would have done
temping.

It would also give her a chance to get to know
Dorothy slowly, she thought, and to find out some
of the secrets that her mother had kept so carefully
for so many years. And it would give her a chance to
get to know Grant much better, too.

'That's fixed, then,' James said. 'There's no need
for you to go down to London at all.'

'Oh, but there is,' she protested. 'I've got appoint-
ments, and mail to check, and I've hardly any clothes
with me, and only a few of my painting materials,
and ... well, I simply must go back fairly soon.'

'Then you simply must come straight back here
again,' Dorothy said. 'James, you could pick Mandy
up at the station again next week, couldn't you? On
Tuesday, say? Or Wednesday?'

'Tuesday I could manage,' James agreed. 'If you
arrived in the late afternoon. Couldn't I, Grant?'

'Perhaps,' Grant said.

Mandy tried to make another protest, but it wasn't
much more than token politeness, and every ar-
gument she made was firmly swept away by James
and Dorothy. 'That's enough,' James finally said. 'It's
fixed now, Mandy, so don't keep on arguing. You'll
tire Dorothy out.'

Dorothy laughed, but Mandy looked across the table with sudden apprehension, and saw that she did indeed look tired. 'Dorothy,' she persisted, 'are you sure this won't be too much for you?'

'Not at all,' Dorothy said firmly. 'But I am rather tired now. James, will you help me get ready for bed? Grant, you won't mind...'

'Not at all. Go right ahead, Dorothy.'

'Pour Mandy some more coffee,' James suggested. 'I'll be back in a quarter of an hour or so, and we can get down to our paperwork then.'

The dining-room door closed behind him and Dorothy, and Grant picked up the coffee-pot.

'Black or white?'

'Black,' she said. She watched him pour it. A whole summer with Grant! she thought, suddenly exultant. Perhaps we'll go out on the river again; perhaps he'll kiss me again, or even...

These thoughts were abruptly wiped away when Grant lifted his face to push her cup across to her, and Mandy took in his cold expression.

'You planned all that very neatly,' he said in a harsh voice.

Dismay swept over her. Oh, no, not more accusations, not more suspicion! He had seemed so friendly earlier; what on earth could have brought all this out again?

'Planned what?' she demanded.

'Your trip to Norwich, your little tale about the gallery owner. The perfect scenery to suit your talents. The perfect job to help set poor little Mandy on to her feet as an artist. Nothing too obvious, but all of it carefully set up to make sure that Dorothy and James would come up with the invitation you wanted.'

'Grant!' she exclaimed in amazement and fury. 'You can't honestly believe that! I never even dreamed that they'd ask me to stay for longer. It never crossed my mind before, honestly. I took it for granted that I'd go back to London at the end of the week. I hadn't packed enough clothes for a longer stay or anything.'

'But you left the offer from the gallery open, even though you knew you wouldn't be able to take it up from London.'

'It isn't a firm offer,' she protested. 'It's true, I didn't tell the man I wouldn't be able to do it, but that was just wishful thinking, not wanting to turn my back on something I'd have liked so much. It wasn't anything more than that, Grant, honestly it wasn't.'

'You can't fool me, Mandy. You know I know damn well why you need some more time at Heron's Nest.'

She frowned. Did he mean he knew about—no, he couldn't! Dorothy hadn't said a word even to her, so she would hardly have confessed her secret to Grant. But what else could he mean? She simply hadn't a clue.

'Grant,' she persisted, 'I haven't the faintest idea what you're talking about.'

Grant didn't seem to hear her. 'I was such a damn fool on that afternoon I saw you here,' he went on, in an angry voice. 'The woman decoy: it's the oldest trick in the burglar's book, isn't it? And I played right into your hands. One look at your pretty face and I never thought to call the police or search the back of the house. I didn't even stay around, I dragged you away with me, and gave your accomplice all the time in the world to get away safely.'

'My accomplice?' A cold weight seemed to sink into her stomach. 'Grant,' she whispered, 'what on earth are you suggesting?'

'Of course,' he went on, 'now you know it'll take longer than you'd originally reckoned, don't you? There's more stuff than you expected, isn't there? And James and Dorothy have swallowed your cover story hook, line and sinker. So you planned to take a whole summer. Check it all out, and make sure you get away with the best. But you won't, Mandy Mason. You won't get away with it, because I'm on to you. And I'm warning you now, I'll unmask you. Come back to this house ever again, and I'll unravel every one of your lies, and show you up for the cheap little fraud you are!'

'Grant, you're insane!'

'I *was* insane—insane ever to trust you for a second. But I see it now, and you'll never fool me again.'

Mandy gazed at him in horror. She didn't understand what he was talking about at all. True, she *had* lied; she *did* have something to hide. But what did her pretence to be Dorothy's cousin instead of her daughter have to do with accomplices and 'getting away with the best'? It made no sense. And it was horrible, horrible that Grant should be talking to her like this!

'You didn't say any of this when James and Dorothy were here,' she said in hopeless confusion.

The look Grant gave her was filled with such contempt that it sickened her to the core. 'How could I? Dorothy is a sick woman. I wouldn't risk upsetting her by telling her what a sordid little thief her "cousin" really is. No, it won't be to Dorothy that I go with the truth when I have it, Mandy, or to James either. As soon as I have you nailed, I'll be taking my evidence straight to the police.'

Thief? Thief! The confusion in Mandy's brain suddenly cleared, blasted away by the brutality of Grant's accusation. Whatever else she was, she was certainly no thief! 'You're crazy, Grant Livingstone!' she cried. 'I *am* Dorothy's relative! And that's the worst thing I ever heard in my life, to have you accuse me of being a thief. You won't get proof of that, you *can't* get proof of it, because it's simply not true!'

She glared at him. And Grant, rising from the table, glared back at her, his flecked hazel eyes holding her own, hypnotically binding. 'Maybe I haven't proved it yet,' he said quietly and dangerously. 'But now you've given me a lot longer to set about finding where you've lied, haven't you, Mandy Mason?'

He turned and strode from the room, and a moment later she heard the sound of his Range Rover crunching on the gravel outside the house. She sat down and buried her head in her hands in sheer despair. Only pride made her keep back the tears until after James had reappeared, and she had managed to stumble out an explanation about an urgent appointment that Grant had forgotten, and the apology he had asked her to give for his sudden departure.

CHAPTER SEVEN

MANDY had a strange dream that night. The woman in the art gallery in Elm Hill was chasing her up the cobbled street, shouting 'Thief! Thief!' at her. Mandy was running away in terror, though she knew in some way that she wasn't guilty of anything, wasn't really a thief. She saw the big tree with the bench round it, and hurled herself towards it as if it would be some kind of sanctuary, and then she realised that Grant was waiting there, and her foot hit a stone, and she tripped . . .

And woke, suddenly, to find herself sitting bolt upright in bed in her darkened room at Heron's Nest.

It hadn't been as frightening as some nightmares, but it had unnerved her, and she didn't feel ready to go back to sleep. Very quietly she got up and slipped her dressing-gown on, and made her way down to the kitchen to get a cup of coffee.

She didn't like to put on the hall and landing lights, and in the gloom of the summer night the pictures made the walls look heavy and misshapen. So many pictures . . .

That was it! Of course. It came to her as she was spooning her coffee into her cup. That was what Grant thought: that she had come to Heron's Nest to steal the pictures!

She had thought it laughable at first, she remembered, when he had suggested she might be masquer-

ading as a relative of Dorothy's in order to penetrate
the house. It wasn't a millionaire's house, she had
thought: the Fernhams were obviously comfortably
off, but they weren't remotely rich enough to justify
the time and trouble that a scheme like that would
take. It had just seemed ridiculous to her.

But the day before, the woman in the gallery had
brought it home to her how valuable Horace
Blackwater's works were. Two hundred and fifty
pounds for a small watercolour that wasn't anything
like his very best! Most of the paintings at Heron's
Nest were much finer, and larger too. And there were
hundreds, if not thousands of them. A couple of
hundred at least were framed on the walls, and in one
of the attics, Dorothy had told her, there were three
cabinets crammed full of unframed watercolours and
ink drawings. There were quite a few oils, too, and
oils always cost much, much more than watercolours;
they were probably worth a thousand pounds or more
each.

It all added up to a fortune. The Fernhams really
were rich, she thought in amazement. Maybe they
weren't millionaires, but their art collection was surely
worth hundreds of thousands of pounds.

Somehow, her unconscious mind had fitted together
the pieces of the jigsaw that her conscious mind that
revolted against—and had shown her exactly what
Grant was thinking. He must have thought that she
knew all about Horace Blackwater, and had discovered what a cache of his work there was at Heron's
Nest. And she had wormed her way into the
Fernhams' lives, he clearly imagined, so that she

would have a chance to evaluate their collection, and steal some of it.

Looked at from his viewpoint, it *did* seem believable, she had to admit. Blackwaters were in such high demand, and the security at Heron's Nest was far from tight. If she really had 'nosed around' the attics, she could have spirited away a dozen paintings—no, a couple of dozen, or even more than that—and her theft might have gone undiscovered for weeks, months or even years. Dorothy wasn't able to go to the upper floors of the house, and Mandy could well believe that neither James nor Mrs Jackson took much interest in the paintings. A simple deception on a crippled woman, and she might have walked away with thousands of pounds' worth of loot.

It was vile, absolutely disgusting. Never in a million lifetimes would she have done any such thing. But other people did, she knew. Perhaps Grant had come across a case like that before; perhaps he knew someone who had been taken in by a convincing conman. And then he had sensed that Mandy had lied—as she had—and his mind had begun to work along these all too likely lines.

Though the thought was horrible, it was a relief to her to come to this conclusion. It all made sense now. She knew what Grant suspected her of—and, just as important, she was reassured that he *didn't* suspect her and Dorothy Fernham's real secret. And it seemed obvious to her what she should do about it. She should go straight to Grant, and explain that she understood now what he had been hinting at, and make things up with him. She wasn't a thief, after all, and if she spoke frankly to him she was sure she would manage to make him understand that.

Much relieved, she drained the last of her coffee, and made her way back to her room, telling herself that she would make an opportunity to talk to him the very next day. ·

In fact, talking to Grant wasn't as easy as she had anticipated. Catwood Wherrymen were in the midst of their busy season, and both he and James seemed to be perpetually hard at work. James was politely dismissive when she suggested calling into the yard on Wednesday, or Thursday, or Friday. He appreciated her interest, he assured her, but really they wouldn't have time to spare for even a cup of coffee with her.

She would have to see Grant one evening, she decided. But this too was difficult, because she didn't want to give Dorothy and James any hint of what she had in mind; or even to give them the wrong impression in other directions, by telling them outright that she planned to call on Grant at his house.

In the end she decided that this was one occasion on which a white lie was justified. She discovered a sudden burning desire to see the film that was showing at the Odeon in Wroxham, luckily one which didn't appeal to Dorothy and James, and assured them that she was perfectly happy to go to the cinema alone.

James offered to lend her his car, but she felt that it wouldn't be fair to accept it, and luckily she didn't need it because she had discovered an old bicycle in one of the outhouses at Heron's Nest. It had once been Dorothy's, she assumed, because it was a woman's model and clearly had not been ridden for many years. An hour's work on Wednesday afternoon—plus an investment in a puncture repair kit and a new set of batteries for the lights—made it usable, and after supper on Wednesday Mandy waved goodbye and set out, with a map of the area in one pocket and a note of Grant's address—secretly copied out of the telephone book—in the other.

It was only about three miles to Grant's house, and she found it without too much difficulty. It was one of a row of modern bungalows that backed—as Mandy had learned from her map—on to the River Bure. She swung her bicycle into the driveway, feeling terribly nervous and wishing that she had decided to phone in advance, after all. What if Grant wasn't in? What if he was in, and Pam, or somebody else, was with him?

She propped the bike up against the garage wall, and looked around her. The bungalow looked to be on the small side but, like several she had seen in the area, it had a very large garden. Lawns, reasonably kept, though not as immaculate as those at Heron's Nest, led the eye down to the river, where there was a wooden landing-stage and a rowing-boat bobbing on the slow-moving water. Of course, she should have known, thought Mandy, that he would have chosen a house with a river frontage on purpose, and would make good use of it.

She took a deep breath, and went to knock on the front door. A moment later a large black shadow loomed up behind the glass of the door, and Grant opened it and stood staring at her.

'I came to see you,' she said unnecessarily.

'So I see. You'd better come in.'

He led her back down the hall, and into a large living-room, with a wall of glass that gave views out down the garden and on to the river beyond.

She gazed around her, unable to rein in her curiosity about Grant's home. It was a pleasant room, comfortably furnished in a rather plain modern style, with a pair of low leather-covered sofas, a coffee-table strewn with newspapers and magazines, and half a dozen pictures on the walls. Something about the room spelled out the fact that it belonged to a bachelor: there were no subtle feminine touches, and everything seemed to be on a large scale, as if it was specifically designed to accommodate Grant's huge frame. But, though neither the room nor the house were self-consciously decorative, Mandy sensed that Grant had chosen everything with great care, and with an eye to its appearance as well as its convenience.

'Seen enough?' Grant said sarcastically.

'I'm sorry,' she responded. She felt a hint of redness rising in her cheeks. 'Look, I know I should have phoned or something, but I thought—well, I have to explain things to you.'

'Sit down,' he said tersely.

He wasn't being welcoming, she thought miserably, or friendly, or remotely trying to put her at her ease. He hadn't even offered her a cup of coffee! She perched on the edge of one of the leather sofas, and wrung her hands together.

'You see,' she began, 'I can see now what you thought about me.'

She stumbled through her story, telling him everything that he didn't already know: all about the other art gallery in Norwich, the one with the Blackwater in the window, about her dream, and about her sudden realisation that he had suspected her of stealing the pictures. She put in plenty of facts, hoping that this would help to convince him that it was all true, and assured him that he was welcome to check with the gallery assistant if he wanted to.

'I might,' Grant said. There was silence for a moment, and Mandy stole a surreptitious glance at him. He too was tensely seated on the edge of a sofa, with his hands clasped together, and his forehead furrowed as if he was thinking over everything she had just told him.

He looked up at her, and said, 'You really expect me to believe that you didn't know about Horace Blackwater before you came to Heron's Nest?'

'I didn't, Grant. Honestly I didn't.' She said it with conviction, since this too was the truth. 'It must be difficult for you to believe that, I can see, because you've obviously known about him for years.' She glanced again about the room. Her first impression hadn't been mistaken: as far as she could judge from a distance, at least two of Grant's pictures were by Blackwater. 'Maybe anyone in Norfolk would, but I'd never been to Norfolk before, Grant. Horace Blackwater may be fairly well-known these days, but he certainly isn't a household name all across the country. You must have mentioned him to strangers before, and drawn a blank.'

'But you're an artist, Mandy.'

'True, but I only had a year's training at art school, and none of my courses covered English water-colourists of between the wars! It's not my field,

Grant, and as far as I know there are very few Black-
waters in the major public collections. I don't think
I'd ever seen one of his works before I came to Heron's
Nest.'

'That's possible,' Grant admitted. 'But there's
something else. Something harder to explain away.
You say you're his great-granddaughter.'

'And that's true as well,' she responded with conviction. 'A great-granddaughter who was brought up
by a stepmother, and never knew any of her real
mother's family at all.'

'So you say.'

Mandy gazed at him in despair. 'Grant, I can't
prove it!' she wailed. 'I can't prove that there wasn't
somebody else lurking in the bushes when you found
me at Heron's Nest! I can't prove that I didn't know
all about Horace Blackwater! I'd find it hard even to
prove beyond all possible doubt that I'm his great-
granddaughter. But for heaven's sake, I shouldn't have
to! And you haven't proved the opposite, either!'

There was a long silence. She tried to catch Grant's
eye, but he wouldn't look at her; he stared down at
his hands, clasped between his spread knees. She
sensed that he was torn, that he was almost ready to
believe her, but that it still needed something else to
persuade him.

She took a brave plunge.

'What made you think it, Grant?' she asked gently.
'What put the idea in your mind?'

He glanced up briefly, and then stood up, and began
to pace about the room.

'James and Dorothy are both so unworldly,' he said
with sudden vehemence, coming to a halt near the

windows. 'They're not business people, they don't think in money terms. It's a struggle, every day, to get James to make sensible decisions about the Wherrymen. I love the wherries too, for heaven's sake, but we can only run them if we make money out of the cruisers! He's so vague, and he's been had before by plausible rogues. And then there was a robbery, a few months ago...'

His voice tailed off, and Mandy sensed, suddenly, that this was something that had come home very hard to him.

'Who was robbed, Grant? James and Dorothy?'

'No.' He looked across at her, and gave an odd, twisted grin. 'I was.'

'What did they take?'

'Paintings.'

'Paintings?'

'You see——' Grant said. He started pacing again. 'I had a little Cotman, a watercolour I'd bought years ago, when I first started work. Not museum stuff, but I thought it was lovely. Cost me the earth, or so it seemed at the time.'

'I can imagine,' Mandy said, surprised. A Cotman! Cotman was the most famous of the Norwich school of painters, and his works went for large sums of money. Much as she loved them, she had never even dreamed of possessing one herself. Grant must have coveted it strongly, and then saved for months to buy it, she thought. No wonder he had taken it hard if it was stolen from him.

'They broke in through the bathroom window, and took that, and a Stannard, not as good as the Cotman but still a very nice piece, and a couple of

Blackwaters.' He glanced at his walls, and then at Mandy again. 'Not these ones: Dorothy gave me these afterwards. I'll never get them back, of course. They'll have disappeared by now into the international art market.' He shook his head. 'I always lock up, of course, but I'd never thought anyone would steal the pictures, never thought I needed burglar alarms and all that junk. Then afterwards I talked to James and Dorothy, just to make sure they had their collection insured, and...'

'And they don't?'

'Now they do, but they're still hopelessly under-insured, I reckon, and Dorothy's never made a proper inventory of the pictures, and their locks are a scandal. Heron's Nest is a leaky sieve of a house, just waiting for an enterprising thief who knows what he's looking for. Or she,' he ended with cruel humour.

'Well,' Mandy said firmly, 'I'm not it. And if I were, Grant, if I really had been planning to dupe Dorothy, don't you think I'd have run a mile as soon as you first hinted that you were on to me? While as it was, I was too dense even to realise what you were getting at until a couple of days ago!'

'That's true,' Grant admitted with a rueful smile. 'That I do believe, now.'

'You believe it all now, surely? You do believe I'm Mandy Mason? That I only came to Heron's Nest to meet Dorothy and James?'

'Give me time.'

Time? She didn't want to give him time, she wanted him to fall on his knees right then and beg her for-giveness! But that wasn't Grant, she thought, with a sudden rush of warmth towards him. He wasn't a man for snap decisions and equally quick repentance. He was somebody who made up his mind slowly, and thought before acting on it. He'd come round, she felt sure, and more than make up for his earlier mistaken suspicions, but he would do it in his own good time.

'Well, while you're thinking about it,' she said teasingly, 'how about a cup of coffee?'

'Impossible woman!' Grant groaned. But he said it with a smile, and promptly made his way to the kitchen.

What a pleasure it was to know that she had finally nailed down the source of Grant's suspicions, and quashed them. Even by the time he returned with two mugs of coffee, Mandy sensed that he had warmed still further to her. She explained how she had told a white lie to Dorothy and James in order to come and explain to him without upsetting them, and he promptly invited her to spend the rest of the evening with him.

'It's too late for the cinema now,' he said, 'but we can check in the local paper to make sure you get back at the right time.'

'Ten-ten,' she responded. 'I already did!'

Grant laughed, and went to put on a record. 'Mozart suit you?'

Mozart did. It suited her very well to sit in Grant's pleasant living-room, and watch the sun going down over the river, and listen to Mozart's gentle, civilised music, and look on Grant's long body, sprawled out on his hearthrug. He was a very secure man, she thought, in spite of the understandable caution that had made him so suspicious of her earlier on. He seemed to have worked out exactly what kind of house he wanted, what pictures, what music—to know just where he belonged.

Mandy sensed that he was very content with his own life: with his work, his home, his friends. But, all the same, it seemed a little odd to her that he wasn't married. He was thirty-three, she knew from Dorothy: and it wasn't that he hadn't settled down, simply that he seemed to have settled down without a permanent woman in his life. Was it just that he hadn't made marriage a priority, she wondered, or was there some psychological reason why he had shied away from a close commitment to one special person?

She didn't like to ask directly, but she did want to know more about him, so she said carefully, 'Do your family live nearby, Grant?'

'My family?' Grant turned on to his side, and gave her a sharp glance, then looked rapidly away again. 'I don't have a family,' he said.

'They're dead, you mean?'

'Oh, they're around somewhere.'

He said it with such casual bitterness that she was shocked for a moment. She didn't want to jar their new friendship by asking offensive questions, but it seemed an awkward moment to change the subject, so she went on, 'You don't see them at all?'

'My parents divorced when I was eight. My dad brought me up after that. Then he got married again, and I left home as soon as I could. He's in Ipswich. My mother tends to move around. I saw her a couple of years ago.'

'You must have been very unhappy.'

'No. I just got used to being alone a lot.'

There was a flat finality in his voice now that warned Mandy off asking any more questions. All the same, she was oddly disturbed by what she had learned. She had imagined that Grant had grown up in enviable security, with that total sense of belonging that she had never really known herself; and instead his childhood sounded as if it had been much more disrupted than hers had! Maybe he did belong in his world now, but he had had to create it for himself, she thought. It wasn't something that he had inherited and now took for granted.

'You see a lot of Dorothy and James?' an impulse made her say.

'I suppose I do.' Grant turned and looked at her again, this time with a more narrowed look. 'James wanted children,' he said bluntly. 'But they didn't come, so he has to make do with me instead. I don't know about Dorothy.'

Nor do I, thought Mandy; nor do I.

'It's not far off ten. I'll make some more coffee, and then I'll take you home.'

'I've a bike with me,' she said, as she followed him into the kitchen. It was neat and well-planned, she saw, like the rest of the house. Grant obviously wasn't a keen cook, but the kitchen looked as if it was used regularly and thoughtfully. She suspected that he liked his food enough to make a reasonable effort to turn out tasty meals when he wasn't invited to eat elsewhere.

'That's OK,' he said. 'It'll fit in the back of the Range Rover, and I'll drop you just up from the house.'

'Thanks.'

It had been an odd evening, she thought, as she and Grant drove back to Heron's Nest in silence. Grant clearly believed her now, and his old antagonism was gone, but, as he had warned her earlier, he was coming round only slowly to a different attitude, and there had been nothing lover-like in his manner towards her. Perhaps he really was committed to Pam? she wondered. She didn't dare to ask him.

He pulled up the Range Rover a short distance down the lane from the house.

'I'll have to bike it at top speed,' she said cheerfully, 'so as to work up a convincing sweat!'

'Dorothy won't look all that hard.'

'True, but that's no excuse for not making an effort. There's always a chance she'd notice if I didn't bother, and I wouldn't want her to realise I'd lied to her.' She hesitated, and added, 'Even in a little thing.'

'So long as that's all it was.'

'It was, Grant. It is.'

'I believe you.' He reached out, very slowly, and drew her towards him.

His kiss began gently, but this time it intensified rapidly and alarmingly, till the two of them were clinging together with blind abandonment. Mandy's mouth opened under the pressure of his, and her tongue sought out and duelled with his in a way that was deeper than any mere causal flirtation. She wanted him, and she wanted him to know it; and at the same time every movement she made was anticipated by his, leaving her in no doubt that he wanted her just as urgently.

His hand traced a warm path down her side, stopping at her waist, loosening her skirt from her jeans, and then working back up beneath it to caress the soft mound of her breast. A confident finger found her nipple, and teased it to aching hardness, and Mandy drew back her mouth just far enough to murmur her pleasure.

'Oh, Mandy, what you do to me!' Grant muttered. His lips and teeth traced a path down the tendon at the side of her neck, and his tongue curled into the hollow of her collarbone.

'Grant, Grant!' She urged her body still closer, mentally cursing whoever had designed the Range Rover and left such a maddening gap between the two front seats.

'I've been aching for this to happen,' he murmured again, bringing his mouth back to hers, and bringing his hand downwards, smoothing it hard against the rough material of her denims.

'Me, too!'

'Not the place for it, though.' A final lingering kiss, and Grant drew back. Cool air seemed to flood between them, spelling out the unwelcome gap between their two bodies.

'I suppose not,' she reluctantly agreed.

'I'll call round before you go down to London.' Grant opened the car door, and went round to the back to get out her bicycle.

'Yes, do.'

'Take care.' He handed over the bike, and bent to deposit one more light kiss on her head. Then he strode back to the driver's seat, and a moment later he was driving off into the dark.

CHAPTER EIGHT

'You're absolutely sure you can manage the wheel-chair, Mandy?' James Fernham persisted, as he drew his car into the forecourt of Catwood Wherrymen.

'Oh, don't be such a fusspot, James,' Dorothy said, in an affectionately scolding voice. 'She's seen you do it a dozen times, and if she can't remember how it unfolds then I can remind her, can't I?'

'And don't keep her out too late,' James continued, cheerfully ignoring his wife. 'She tires more easily than she'll admit, even sitting in the car. Back home by four-thirty, OK?'

'OK, James,' agreed Mandy. 'I'll have Dorothy back by mid-afternoon, then I'll come to fetch you at what—five-thirty?'

'No need, Grant can give me a lift. I think. Hold on a minute.' James got out of the car, slammed the door, and disappeared towards the office.

Dorothy half turned her head—a slow and, Mandy feared, rather painful operation—and looked at Mandy, who was sitting in the back of the car. 'Don't mind James fussing,' she said. 'He knows we'll be all right.'

'So do I,' Mandy replied. It was true. She had helped Dorothy into and out of her wheelchair often in the ten days since she had returned to Heron's Nest for the second time, and she had driven James's Volvo estate into Wroxham the previous evening, so she was familiar with the feel of the big car.

She turned from Dorothy and saw James coming back towards them, with Grant just a pace behind him. James reached to the passenger door by Mandy, and opened it. 'OK, young lady. In the driver's seat. And Grant will bring me home.'

'Drive carefully,' Grant said. 'Try to keep to the main roads, there's not much passing space for a big car on the country lanes. And go gently on the gear changes. The clutch needed looking at last time I drove this heap, and I bet James hasn't had it done yet.'

'This *heap*?' James exploded. 'Calling my precious Volvo a heap, just because it's a year or two older than your Range Rover!' He grinned. 'Actually you're only too right, Grant. I really ought to take it into the garage.'

After a couple more friendly exchanges, and a pause for Mandy to adjust the driver's seat and mirrors, they were on their way. Dorothy directed her along the road that led north-east from Wroxham and Stalham, and then to the coast at Sea Palling.

'There's nothing to see there but sand dunes,' she said, 'but I like the drive, and I quite like the sand dunes too. Then if we've time we can perhaps go on up the coast to Happisburgh. There's a lighthouse there.'

'Fine,' Mandy said. 'Would you like the radio on?'

Dorothy agreed, and Mandy turned the knobs until classical music flooded out into the car. It wouldn't be any great loss, she thought, that they couldn't easily talk over the music. By now she had come to accept the fact that Dorothy wasn't to be prodded about personal matters. Perhaps she would talk of them one day, Mandy hoped, but it would be she who chose the time and the place.

Sea Palling proved to be as plain a seaside resort as Dorothy had said. Mandy pulled up the car in a car park just out of sight of the sea, and after a short struggle with the collapsible wheelchair she wheeled Dorothy over the slope that led to the beach.

'No further,' Dorothy said, when they reached the bottom. 'It's next to impossible to push this thing over sand. Just move me out of the way of people coming down.'

Mandy did so. The beach wasn't crowded; it was a pleasant day, but not particularly warm, and it wasn't yet the school summer holidays. She sat down beside Dorothy on the sand, and they stayed silent for a long time, looking out at the sea.

'I should never have called you Susannah,' Dorothy said suddenly.

Mandy turned to her. A sudden nervous excitement bubbled inside her. This is it, she thought. She's going to tell me now.

'Why not? I think it's a very pretty name.'

'Oh, it is. It was my grandmother's name. But you're Mandy now: I should have accepted that.'

Mandy hesitated, then she said slowly, 'I never really knew who I was, Dorothy. My parents—the Masons, I mean—brought me up to know I was adopted. Beth couldn't have children of her own, and they made a big thing about how they'd chosen me specially. I think I accepted that all right until I was eleven or so. But then I began to get self-conscious about it, and I wouldn't talk about it any more, and I began to wonder more and more what my real parents were like. Beth and Bert are good people, but I'm nothing like either of them. I don't look like them, or think like them either.'

Dorothy gave her a taut sideways look. 'You're less like me than I'd expected,' she said, with the odd touch of brutality that her conversation often showed when neither James nor Grant was there. 'It's true, you're very like Frances when she was a girl, but I can't see myself in you, or your father either.'

Mandy managed to give a painful grin. 'That's perhaps as well.'

'Perhaps it is.' Dorothy took a deep breath, and then she went on in a rush, 'I know you don't like knowing that James doesn't know. But I never told him before, and it's too late now.'

'Look,' Mandy said awkwardly, 'you mustn't feel that you have to tell me any of this.'

'But I must,' Dorothy persisted. 'It's only fair. You have to know as much as I can tell you, it's only right.'

'I already know so much more than I'd expected to. You, the house, Horace Blackwater's pictures—they've all changed my idea of myself.'

'But you should know the rest,' Dorothy insisted. She gave a little sigh, and moved her body slightly in the wheelchair. 'I was very young,' she said a moment later. 'Younger than you are now. Eighteen when you were born.'

She fell silent, as if she was remembering. Mandy waited for a few moments, then she prompted, 'Was I born in Little Catwood?'

'Oh, no!' Dorothy exclaimed. 'It would hardly be a secret if you had been. No, you were born in London, in a clinic.'

It sounded rather prosaic. But she hadn't been looking for fairy-tales, she reminded herself firmly: simply for the truth. 'So your parents sent you down...'

Dorothy sighed again. 'It happened in Italy. I told you, I was planning to be an artist too, and when I left school my parents arranged for me to go to Florence. My grandfather knew lots of people in Italy, so they sent me to stay with the family of one of his old friends. I was supposed to live there for a year before I went to art school, to learn Italian, and look at the masterpieces, and do a little painting.'

'But you didn't stay?'

'Oh, for long enough. Long enough for it to happen, at least.' She paused, then went on, in a harsh voice, 'It was nothing like Norfolk. I got involved with your father without really realising what was happening. He was an artist of sorts, and it all seemed so romantic, falling in love in Florence. He was in his late twenties, but somehow it never occurred to me that he might be married. It turned out he'd always assumed that I knew he was. So had Signora Rossi. I'd even met his wife, though I hadn't realised who she was. I met so many people, and my Italian wasn't good, so I didn't place half of them. The Rossis were horrified when they found out.'

'How awful for you,' Mandy murmured.

'It served me right,' said Dorothy brusquely. 'Oh, I was young, but I was stupid too. I wouldn't admit to myself that everything wasn't as perfect as I wanted it to be. I should have seen what was happening, that's obvious to me now. I was foolish and blind, and I wrecked my life and yours too.'

Mandy clenched her fist around a handful of sand. It seemed to her that Dorothy was deliberately telling the story brutally, with no softening explanations, no touches that might beg her own sympathy. She wanted to say the right things, but she didn't feel sympathetic, just . . . shaken. It was like, and yet unlike, what she had expected to hear. It was romantic in a way: Florence, an artist, an eager young English girl, and yet Dorothy seemed to be going out of her way to make it sound sordid.

'You mustn't think that, Dorothy,' she made herself say. 'You must have suffered so much when you gave me up, but I wasn't hurt, I promise you. The Masons have been wonderful parents, I couldn't have asked to belong to a nicer family. Beth would never be anything but grateful that you gave her the chance to bring up a child, and I've no cause to criticise you either.'

Dorothy didn't respond to this effort; she seemed to be wrapped up in her memories. 'Of course it was all hushed up,' she went on, a moment later. 'The Rossis told my parents, and they worked out a tale about an illness which forced me to go back to England. Then I stayed in London until after you were born, and afterwards I went to college in London, and I didn't come back to Heron's Nest until after I graduated.'

And then you met James again, Mandy thought, and married him.

'You never thought of telling James?'

'I thought of it, but I never brought myself to do it. He wouldn't have understood what it had been like in Florence. And by then it was three years since it had happened, and I was used to keeping it to myself.'

'I can understand that.'

'I know it was wrong of me,' Dorothy went on, with sudden vehemence. 'I know I should have told him before we were married. But I didn't do it then, and now I can't, can I?'

'Why not?'

'Because of this, for heaven's sake!' Dorothy banged at the wheelchair with an impatient fist, to make it clear what she meant.

'I can't see that that makes any difference,' persisted Mandy.

'Of course it does. He might hate me for it, but he wouldn't be able to say so, because I'm ill. He couldn't leave me, couldn't divorce me. He's stuck with me now.'

Mandy was appalled at the viciousness of both word and sentiment. 'But he loves you, Dorothy,' she protested.

'Oh, he's put up with it. He's been marvellous, I know. But how could I ask him to put up as well with a guilty secret that I've kept from him for over sixteen years?'

The bitterness in her voice astonished Mandy. She hadn't been under any illusions that Dorothy had found it easy to resign herself to her fate, but it had never really struck her that the disease would have caused serious problems in her marriage. James was such a charming, caring man, and he seemed so devoted to Dorothy. He was the sort of person who would take it for granted that marriage was meant to endure in sickness as well as in health: he surely wouldn't have thought of it as 'putting up'!

No, it wasn't so much James's attitude that was the problem, she thought, as Dorothy's own. What was she? Thirty-seven? She was still young. She had been a passionate young girl, and had plunged headlong into a disastrous affair with a married Italian. She had given birth to her child alone in London, and had had to give it up for adoption. Her life had been blighted by her terrible illness, and there had been no more children. Add to that a husband who was admirable but perhaps not emotionally exciting, and it would be hard, Mandy realised, to keep the recipe from spelling disaster.

Perhaps the Fernhams' marriage wasn't as tranquil as it seemed on the surface, she thought to herself. Come to that, perhaps she was being naïve in thinking that James would take the news well. Dorothy knew him infinitely better than she did herself. It was true, he *had* lived a sheltered life. Maybe he didn't have the emotional resources to cope with such a bombshell.

'I don't believe he would hate you for it, Dorothy,' she said cautiously. 'But if you'd prefer him not to know, then I'll accept that.'

'Fair enough.' Dorothy gave a wry smile. 'It would have been easier if we'd had children ourselves. But we didn't, and now there's no hope.'

'I'm so sorry, Dorothy. I really am.'

'It's not your problem,' Dorothy retorted. 'It's mine. We should be getting back now.'

They made their way back to the car in silence, and barely broke it on the drive back to Heron's Nest. Mandy's head was full of Dorothy's revelations. She was very conscious, too, of Dorothy sitting next to her. Dorothy had talked unexpectedly freely, after her earlier reticence, and yet she still seemed like a stranger. The conversation should have brought them closer, thought Mandy, but it hadn't, not yet.

It was almost five o'clock by the time she had Dorothy back inside Heron's Nest.

'You'll want to rest,' she said, 'before supper.'

Dorothy shook her head. 'I can't right now. Later, maybe. There are some more things I want to show you. Come on through.'

She took the wheels of her chair decisively in her hands, and propelled herself rapidly towards her bedroom. Mandy hadn't been in the room before, and she followed a little apprehensively. She found it to be much like the rest of the ground floor of Heron's Nest. A few pieces of furniture left plenty of room for Dorothy to manoeuvre, and the walls were crammed with more pictures of the Broads.

'You'll have to look for me,' Dorothy said. 'I can't reach it easily. It's all in the bottom drawer of the chest.'

'This chest?' asked Mandy, pointing to a big oak chest that stood in front of the window.

'That's it. On the right-hand side, I think.'

Mandy knelt on the thick carpet, and pulled the drawer open. It was stiff, and she tugged hard until it came out suddenly. Inside, it was full of books and box-files, neatly piled up.

'There's a big file that says "Blackwater" on the spine,' Dorothy said. 'Yes, that one. Take that, and the two albums above it. You'll find all the old family photos and papers in those. I want you to look at them, then some of them should be yours to keep.'

'Oh, no,' Mandy protested. 'These are your things, I can't take them from you.'

'Nobody else need know. Nobody but me ever looks at them.'

Mandy hesitated. 'I would like to look,' she said at last.

'Take them up to your room.'

Mandy nodded. 'Would you like me to stay with you for a while?'

'No, leave me alone now.'

In the end Mandy took only a very short look at the file and albums that day: Grant came back with James, stayed on to supper and lingered afterwards. Then, in the days that followed, they largely slipped her mind.

She took a small batch of her watercolours into Norwich to show Mr Myers, the gallery owner, and to her delight he agreed to show them. James and Dorothy directed her to another gallery in Cromer, and she took the train up to the north coast resort, returning overjoyed with another small order. There was a series of fine days, and much of the time she spent cycling around the Broadland and finding places to sketch.

She saw Grant several times, and their relationship steadily deepened, but slowly. He wasn't a man to rush things, she sensed, and though his attraction to her

was obviously powerful he still seemed to be holding
back from any kind of emotional commitment.
Mandy wasn't sorry. This kind of relationship was a
new thing for her too, and she was glad to be able to
take her time over it.

She was very conscious of Dorothy's attitude, too,
and she didn't want to fuel her mother's jealousy.
Dorothy was only a few years older than Grant, after
all. It wouldn't be easy, Mandy sensed, for her to
switch from thinking of him as a special friend to
seeing him as the lover of her unacknowledged
daughter.

Almost a fortnight after the trip with Dorothy,
Mandy found herself alone one evening. James and
Dorothy had been invited out to dinner with friends,
and Mandy had assured them that she was happy to
stay at the house. She had been hoping that Grant
would come round, but he hadn't phoned, and there
were no programmes she wanted to watch on the television. She read half-heartedly through a couple of
chapters of a paperback, then suddenly remembered
the albums.

She brought them down to the living-room, since
the light was better than in her bedroom, and cautiously opened them. On second thoughts she brought
down her family-tree folder too, so that she would be
able to check who was who among her new-found
relations.

The file was a curious mish-mash of official and
personal papers: birth, marriage and death certifi-
cates for generations of the Blackwater family, details
of a long-past lawsuit over some property in the
village—she skipped quickly over these—and a couple

of sheaves of letters. She untied the ribbon fastening one of them, and quickly realised that they were love-letters. 'My darling George,' she read. Who was George? Presumably Dorothy's father, George Blackwater.

She set these aside, wondering if she should read them later, and then turned to the second sheaf. The writing on the first envelope was oddly familiar, and when she extracted the letter she realised why: it was Horace Blackwater's handwriting, which she knew from the captions on his watercolours. The letter was to his son, written when he was in Italy himself, and talking largely about his and other people's paintings.

Most of the other letters in this batch were similar, letters from Horace to other family members, mainly about his work. Mandy found them fascinating. Horace had had both a strong painter's eye for land-scape, and a clear turn of phrase. Reading the letters, it was almost as if the scenes he saw, and the pictures he planned to base on them, were in front of her. She read on, absorbed.

The doorbell took her by surprise. Had Dorothy or James forgotten something? she wondered. She dropped the pile of letters on her lap on to a heap on the floor, and went to answer it.

'Grant!' she cried, reaching out to hug him on the doorstep. 'I'd decided you weren't coming.'

'I only left the yard a few minutes ago,' he said, dropping a gentle kiss on her hair and following her into the house. 'I thought of phoning, but you said you'd be in anyway, so...'

'So you decided to risk finding me washing my hair.'

'I know you better than that. You always wash it
in the mornings.'

'So I do.' She grinned. 'Actually, I was...' Actually, she would much prefer Grant not to see the
photograph albums and papers, she suddenly thought,
because he still didn't know—and wasn't to know—
that she was Dorothy's daughter and not Frances's.

'Watching a trashy soap opera?'

'Wrong night for them. No, I was looking at some
old family albums that Dorothy showed me. I'll just
put them away, and we can talk and perhaps put on
some music.'

'Oh, don't put them away yet,' said Grant, coming
into the living-room, and seeing the pile on the floor.
'I'd be interested to see them too.'

'If you're sure. I don't want to bore you. But these
are fascinating, really—they're Horace Blackwater's
letters to his son. Look at this one, it's all about his
paintings of Verona. You know there's one of them
on the landing, the big one on the far wall.'

'Really?' Grant said enthusiastically. He bent down
to take the letter from Mandy, then settled in one of
the armchairs and began to read it.

She watched him for a moment. She could share
this part of Dorothy's offering happily with him, she
thought. He knew she was Horace Blackwater's great-
granddaughter: it was a relationship she was free to
acknowledge, and one she was very glad to. Grant
admired her great-grandfather too, and she already
knew that he could talk interestingly and knowl-
edgeably about painting.

How glad she was that he had come, she thought,
watching him turn over the fragile pages with a del-

icacy that seemed remarkable in such a big man. What a pleasure it was to look at his clear profile, the light reflecting on his reddish hair, the strong lines of his body folded into the low chair.

'I'll make us some coffee,' she said. 'I'll be back in a moment.'

She hummed to herself as she made up a tray with coffee-cups, sugar and milk, and carried it back into the living-room. He looked up at her as she pushed the door to behind her, and smiled.

'This is wonderful stuff. I had no idea that Dorothy had any of Horace's letters. She ought to show them to an expert, even think of getting them published, perhaps.'

'That's a good idea. I'll have to suggest it to her.'

Grant set the letter down, and reached for one of the coffee-cups. 'Out of sheer curiosity, though, I'd rather see the photos of your mother.'

'My mother? Oh, yes,' she said quickly, her heart sinking. It was the last thing she wanted, to have to start lying her way through the Blackwater family albums, but she didn't dare to show any reluctance.

'Was she really so like you?'

'I think so, from the photograph I'd seen before, but I haven't had a chance to look through all these yet.'

'Let's have a look together, then. If you don't mind, that is. I'd understand if you'd rather look through them on your own.'

Would he? she wondered. Perhaps he thought he would, but she couldn't help feeling that he would be resentful, perhaps even suspicious, if she did admit to wanting to look alone. So she said, 'Not at all,' and picked one of them up, coming with it to sit at Grant's feet. 'Let's see, Frances Blackwater...'

They hunted all through the albums, but there were only a couple of photographs of Frances, both of them rather blurred.

'Her hair isn't really like yours,' Grant said thoughtfully, his eyes moving from the girl on the photograph to the real one sitting by him. 'It's the same colour, but it doesn't look as curly as yours.'

'Not as wild,' she grinned, shaking out her unruly locks.

'Not as pretty,' Grant said firmly. He reached out to stroke her hair, then caught a hank of it in his hand, and gently pulled her towards him.

Mandy had to get up on to her knees to reach for his kiss. She moved closer, bringing her body between Grant's open legs, and reaching upwards with her hands to pull his head down to her. Their mouths touched softly, and then harder, and Grant brought his hands around her back, pulling her upwards to sit astride him.

'For once,' he murmured, when his mouth was free, 'I've caught you wearing a skirt.'

'So you have.' His hands were proving it, tracing a path up her bare legs, and moving to caress the tender skin of her inner thighs.

'You ought to do it more often.'

'Not very practical.'

'Nonsense,' he laughed. 'I think it's very practical.' His hands cupped her buttocks under the skirt, squeezing gently, and his tongue, probing and teasing her mouth in between his words, reinforced his erotic message.

'Mmm,' Mandy murmured. Grant's hands were doing strange things to her, arousing a warm ache inside her that was crying out for him to keep touching her, more and more intimately. He moved on the big chair, gently trapping her beneath his big body, and then pulling her hard against him so that her breasts were crushed against his firm chest, and her thighs were wrapped around one of his. Her breath seemed to be coming in little pants, and she strained closer to him, revelling in the harsh brush of his cheek as his mouth drifted downwards past her jawline.

'Oh, Mandy...' he whispered. He deposited a trail of kisses around the neck of her T-shirt, and then, to her surprise, began to ease away from her.

'Grant?' she said uncertainly.

'My self-control isn't limitless,' Grant said in a gruff voice. 'I think it's time for more coffee.'

He was right, she supposed: they were in the Fernhams' living-room, after all, and Dorothy and James might return at any moment. But *her* self-control had disappeared even faster than his, and she knew she wouldn't have stopped him if he had taken things further.

'I'll make it,' she said unsteadily.

'Good girl.'

She only remembered when she reached the kitchen that she had left Grant once more with the photograph albums. Would he look through them on his own? she wondered, uneasily. She wished she had had a chance to check their contents, and make sure that there wasn't anything in them that would give the lie to her and Dorothy's little story, and that there weren't any inconsistencies between them and her own family-tree folder.

Apparently there wasn't, though, because when she returned she found Grant absorbedly, and unworriedly, leafing through one of the albums, with Mandy's family-tree chart spread out on the carpet in front of him.

'Anything else interesting?' she asked, in as bright a voice as she could manage.

'Not to me, to be honest.' He gave her a quick smile, and shut the album, putting it back with the others on the floor, and folding the chart back into a neat square. 'My fascination with the Blackwaters isn't endless.'

'You're not one of them, after all.'

'And you are.' Grant gave her a loving look. 'It means a lot to you, doesn't it, to discover all these new relations?'

'Yes, it does,' she said sincerely. 'You can understand that, surely: how important it is to feel you belong to a family, to people, to a place?'

'I can,' Grant agreed. 'Was your stepmother rotten to you?'

'Not rotten, no. Not at all. She was a very good mother, but she and I aren't remotely alike. She's a small neat woman, while I'm...'

'Big and wild,' teased Grant.

'*You* call *me* big?' she retorted. 'Against you I feel tiny and feminine! But I *am* bigger and wilder than Beth, and in a way that made us both uncomfortable.'

'What about your father?'

'Oh, he's OK,' Mandy said awkwardly. How difficult this was, she thought unhappily. She really wanted to share confidences with Grant, to talk honestly to him, and because of Dorothy's determination to keep her secret she wasn't able to tell him the truth, and had to keep on with these stupid half-lies.

What if things between them ever did go further? she thought apprehensively. Would Dorothy allow her to tell him then? She couldn't imagine the alternative. He could hardly meet Beth and Bert without knowing who they really were, and she wouldn't be able to keep him from them forever. They were her family too, in a very real sense, and they would want to know Grant just as he, she hoped, would want to know them. Nor did she want to keep anything secret from him indefinitely. It corrupted things in a way, she felt, just as she felt that Dorothy's secret had corrupted her mother's relationship with James Fernham.

'Not much of a man with kids?' Grant persisted.

'Not really that type, no. Hey,' she said, 'it's nearly ten o'clock. Shall we watch the news on television?'

'Fancy you remembering,' Grant teased. He always liked to watch the late news, she knew by now, so the suggestion struck him as a thoughtful reminder, not an awkward attempt to change the subject.

'I'll put it on now, so we don't miss the start.'

Grant moved over to the sofa to sit by her side, and slipped an arm around her shoulder, drawing her close to him. She snuggled in, relieved that once again she seemed to have escaped from a potentially difficult situation, and they were dozing in front of a late-night movie when Dorothy and James returned home an hour later.

CHAPTER NINE

'I THOUGHT we'd have a dinner party on Saturday,' Dorothy said a few days later over breakfast.

'Good idea,' James agreed. 'The usual crowd? The Tuddenhams, and Grant, and...'

'That's right. Valerie and Mike, and Grant, and Pam Austin, and then I thought I'd invite George Wilkinson to make the numbers up. He's our family doctor, Mandy. You haven't met him yet, have you?'

Mandy went cold inside, but she managed to say, 'No, I haven't,' in a rather strangled voice.

'Sounds fine,' James agreed. 'You'll like George, Mandy. He's young, only in his mid-twenties, and lively by local standards. Full of bright new ideas about preventive medicine.'

'How interesting,' she muttered.

'Can I leave you to check with Grant, then?' Dorothy asked James. 'Tell him Saturday about eight. I'll call Pam myself, but I dare say he'll be bringing her with him.'

'I'll try and remember this morning,' James agreed. 'Mind, check with me this evening just in case I forget!'

'I will.'

James deposited a kiss on his wife's forehead, grabbed the morning paper, and disappeared. Mandy found herself staring at Dorothy, who was calmly buttering another slice of toast. Did she do that on purpose? she thought angrily. Or can she really not have noticed how I feel about Grant?

A third possibility slipped into her mind a moment later. Was Dorothy, perhaps, using this to warn her not to become too involved with Grant, because he was already committed to Pam? He couldn't be! she thought miserably. But she had to admit to herself that he had never said anything to her which would directly contradict that possibility.

'Finished so soon?' Dorothy said, looking up as Mandy's chair scraped on the floor.

'It's a fine morning. I don't want to waste any painting time.'

'You'll be back for lunch?'

'I expect so.'

All Dorothy's guests accepted their invitations, Mandy learned, and in the days that followed neither Dorothy or James made any further mention of Grant or Pam Austin. The yard was still extremely busy, and Mandy knew that Grant was working late most evenings, so it wasn't a surprise that he didn't call at Heron's Nest.

It was a disappointment to her, though. She tried to keep telling herself that she had no claims on him, but that didn't seem to correspond with the way her heart was reacting at all.

She offered to help Dorothy with the dinner party preparations, but Dorothy briskly refused, telling her to concentrate on her painting, and assuring her that she and Mrs Jackson could easily handle it. That was evidently true; Heron's Nest always ran smoothly, and the two of them worked out a careful menu that could almost all be prepared in advance.

Mandy's wardrobe generally worked smoothly, too; she was used to picking out her outfits quickly and confidently, but on Saturday evening she found herself up in her bedroom, dithering hopelessly between two dresses. Should she wear her red jersey, cut on the bias, low at the neck, and dipping diagonally down to a ragged hem? Or the dove-grey silk with a gently bloused top? The red was newer, while the silk on careful inspection looked rather like the second-hand bargain it had actually been. But the red was rather daring, she knew, for the sort of party that Dorothy had in mind.

Oh, Mandy, go out fighting, she told herself. She picked up the red, and shook it down over her head before she could have second thoughts. Worn without an underslip, the jersey clung to her curves. Sophisticated glamour wasn't her normal style, but she felt she looked rather dashing as she peeped into the long mirror on the wardrobe door. She even tried putting her hair up, but all her fingers seemed to have turned to thumbs, and finally she settled for leaving it flying loose around her shoulders. Thin gold chains around her neck and wrists gave the finishing touch.

'Sensational,' was James's verdict when she ventured downstairs.

'Not *too* sensational, I hope?'

'Not at all. George will be knocked out, I bet.'

It's not George I want to knock out, she thought silently, but she smiled, and accepted James's offer of a pre-dinner sherry.

The Tuddenhams appeared very promptly at eight o'clock—as they should, they pointed out, since they were near neighbours—and ten minutes later George

Wilkinson followed them. He turned out to be a slight
man with a mongrel face; hardly the human dynamo
that James had suggested, but very pleasant and
friendly. Then a long time went by before the doorbell
rang again.

Mandy tensed as she listened to James opening the
door. She could hear Pam's voice in the hall, clear
and bell-like, apologising for their being late, with
many giggles, James's polite assurances that they
hadn't delayed dinner, and just a murmur from Grant
that she couldn't catch.

They didn't really sound like a couple, it was only
because they had arrived together, Mandy tried to tell
herself, turning to Valerie Tuddenham and pretending desperately that she had been listening to what
Valerie was saying to her. Then Pam and Grant walked
in, with James following just behind them.

Pam was even prettier than she had appeared from
a distance, with a pert, upturned nose and very white
teeth. She was wearing a yellow dress, high-necked
but tight-fitting, that made Mandy instantly glad she
had chosen her red outfit. Grant was in a dark suit,
looking tall and broad-shouldered and confidently
handsome. He met Mandy's eyes, and she looked
back, conscious of Pam's hawkish gaze, and gave him
a bright smile.

At dinner she was seated between Grant and Mike
Tuddenham, and she determinedly devoted almost all
her attention to Mike, chatting away about the
Norfolk scenery she'd discovered, and about the
gallery owners she had met. Grant joined in once or
twice, and Mandy was conscious that he was half listening to her, but he talked mainly to Dorothy, on his

other side. Pam tried regularly to catch his attention, and he always responded, but with no particular show of enthusiasm as far as Mandy could tell.

After coffee they moved slowly back into the drawing-room. It was still barely dusk outside, and she drifted over to the windows, with a half-formed idea that she'd let the others sit before selecting her own place.

'Come for a walk?' a voice said behind her.

She turned, as slowly as she could manage, to face Grant.

'We really couldn't . . .'

'Of course we could,' Grant said firmly. 'There's something I want to show you.'

He took her arm, and drew her over to Dorothy, murmuring an explanation of sorts before leading her out through the door and hall.

It was cool outside, and Mandy had to keep herself from shivering as Grant's firm grip guided her across the lawns and down towards the waters of the broad. He moved sideways across the lawn, leading her out of sight of the drawing-room windows, towards the kitchen gardens and a narrow path that led through a band of trees and towards the grounds of the neighbouring house.

He stopped abruptly at the side of the path, a couple of paces from the water's edge, and turned round to face her.

'What did you want me to see?' she asked edgily.

Grant gave a very slow smile that creased the skin around his dark-flecked eyes, and darkened their expression.

'Oh, dozens of things,' he said. 'I wanted you to see the very last of the setting sun, striking across the water. I wanted you to see where the moorhens nest in the reeds. I wanted you to see the place just beyond the woods where I found a kingfisher last summer. I've been watching out for it this year, but I've had no luck yet. I wanted to show you a clump of orchids deep in the woods. The ground's a little marshy there, but it's forbidden to pick them, so you can only see them if you're willing to get your feet muddy.'

'That's why you brought me out here?' asked Mandy, as lightly as she could manage.

'Not only that. I brought you here mainly for this.'

His arms reaching out for her, his mouth moving to kiss her, his body settling against hers, were all slow and deliberate, giving her plenty of time to react. And she did. As surely and inevitably as if she had been hypnotised, she found her arms moving around him to tighten their embrace, her mouth opening under his.

They stood there in the half-dark for several minutes after the kiss had ended, arms around each other, enjoying the quiet moment.

'I've never met a woman who made me feel like this before,' Grant said softly.

'Not Pam?' she shot back, rather wickedly.

'Heavens, no! I could have cursed James when he asked me to bring her, but I knew she'd not misinterpret it. We've known each other too well, for too long, to have any illusions on that score. Pam's a pleasant companion, but I'm not looking for more than that from her, and she knows it. I only hoped you'd take it the same way. I wished I could have had a chance to have a word with you beforehand, but I just don't seem to have stopped at work this week.'

'I did wonder,' she admitted.

'You must know you've been on my mind ever since the moment I first saw you.'

He bent to kiss her again: a gentle, sensuous kiss that was filled with love and longing. It felt like magic: the setting, the man, his touch, everything was perfection. She melted into the embrace, moving sensuously against him and glorying in the sheer size and strength of him. The heat seemed to be rising through her body, infusing her skin so that every touch of his hand, his arm, his mouth on her bare shoulders and arms felt like a fiery brand, and she was conscious of the growing arousal in him too.

'Oh, my love,' Grant whispered. Slowly, with obvious reluctance, he loosened his arms. 'To think I was ever stupid enough to mistrust you!'

'It was understandable,' Mandy assured him.

'It was crazy of me,' Grant insisted. 'But you make me crazy, Mandy. You make me feel and want in ways I didn't know I could.'

'I feel the same,' she responded quietly.

'I know.' There was no arrogance in his words, just calm confidence. 'We should be getting back.'

The sun had all but disappeared, and the air felt suddenly cool on her bare arms. She didn't protest as Grant guided her back along the path that edged the water. 'You're cold,' he said a moment later. 'Wait a moment.' He shrugged off his jacket, and set it around her shoulders.

It felt nice. The lining was smooth and silky, and the whole jacket somehow had a feel, a faint, warm spicy smell of Grant about it. She wished for a tri-umphant moment that Pam could see her, though she knew that, with the lights on in the drawing-room, nobody inside would be able to see out clearly. Anyway, that was cruel of her, she told herself. Perhaps Grant truly thought that Pam was indifferent to him, but Mandy had seen the looks Pam had given him over the dinner-table, and suspected that that was at least partly wishful thinking.

Grant rang the following morning. 'I can't come over today,' he told Mandy, 'because I promised to skipper the *Grey Lady* for a group of day-trippers. But I can manage Tuesday evening, if you're not busy?'

'Busy?' she exclaimed, in a voice that told him that nothing, but nothing, would have made her too busy to see him again.

'Dinner, then? I'll pick you up around seven-thirty, and take you somewhere special.'

'Fine,' she agreed. Her heart seemed to be racing as she put down the phone. Somewhere special! At last she seemed to have broken through all Grant's reserves, and she sensed that their relationship was moving into a new, and much deeper, phase.

Her second thoughts, though, brought more mixed feelings in their wake. If she and Grant really were becoming serious about each other, she thought, then she would simply have to tell him the truth about her relationship with Dorothy Fernham. There wasn't any alternative. She couldn't keep up her little lie forever, and, the longer she left it, the more fibs she would have to tell, and the harder it would be eventually to tell him the truth and ask him to forgive them all.

She didn't feel that she could possibly tell him without Dorothy's permission, though, and with a stomach full of butterflies she went off in search of her mother.

She found Dorothy out on the terrace, sorting over a pile of roses that Mrs Jackson had cut, ready to arrange in a couple of tall white vases.

'Grant asked me to go out to dinner with him on Tuesday,' she said, slipping into one of the terrace's wrought-iron chairs. 'I hope you don't mind, Dorothy?'

'Out to dinner?' Dorothy echoed sharply.

'I thought you'd have noticed, well, that I've been seeing quite a lot of Grant, and...' Her voice trailed away in her embarrassment at the expression on Dorothy's face.

'Oh,' Dorothy said. She picked up another rose, and began to snap the thorns off the stem. 'We've no plans for Tuesday,' she said in a curt voice.

'Then that'll be all right?'

Mandy didn't get an answer. Dorothy really was surprised, she thought to herself; she hadn't looked at all, hadn't noticed how things were. I was completely wrong when I wondered if she'd invited Pam to warn me off. It wasn't that at all. She simply hadn't stopped to think that I might be interested in Grant myself.

Dorothy wouldn't protest, she knew. Whining wasn't Dorothy's style. She would hide any hurt she felt as best she could, but she clearly wouldn't welcome the relationship. That made things even more difficult, Mandy thought to herself. If she explained right then what she wanted to tell Grant and why, she would not only be asking something else difficult of Dorothy, but she would also be underlining how far things had already gone between the two of them.

She couldn't do that. She felt that it was only too understandable, even if it was annoying at times, that Dorothy's illness should have made her rather self-centred, and that it was hard for her to see other people's lives clearly. It was understandable, too, that a woman still in her thirties might find it hard to come to see her daughter as a grown-up person with grown-up needs and relationships. Mandy had to accept that, and to make allowances for it. Anyway, it wasn't really important, she told herself. The important thing was that her mother was making real efforts to bring her into her life, and keep her there: that she was facing up to the old pain of the adoption, and slowly coming to terms with it.

Give her time, she thought, and she'll accept my involvement with Grant, and she'll realise that I have no alternative but to tell him the truth. She won't force me to repeat the mistakes that have blighted her life; she'll let us start on our relationship with a clean slate. But I have to give her the time she needs, or I'll wreck everything.

'Would you like some help with the roses?' she asked gently.

'I need a couple more white ones for this arrangement. Could you go and cut them for me? The secateurs are on the bench over there.'

'Of course,' replied Mandy, glad to have made her decision, and to have taken things at least a tiny bit further in the right direction.

*   *   *

It was eight o'clock on Tuesday before Grant arrived at Heron's Nest, but Mandy wasn't alarmed at his lateness; she knew from James that they had had a difficult day with the boats. One of their cruisers had been grounded on a sandbank in Breydon Water, and Grant had spent hours, she knew, arranging for it to be refloated and making alternative plans for the stranded holidaymakers.

He was tired; that was obvious from her first sight of him. Edgy, too. It must have been a wearing time, she thought. He threw himself so intensely into his work that he inevitably took it hard when things went badly. She offered to postpone their date until a different evening, but Grant insisted that they should still go out, and since he had already showered and changed she didn't persist.

'I'm taking you to an Italian restaurant in Aylsham,' he said. 'There's nowhere much to eat in Wroxham itself. It'll be less than a twenty-minute drive.'

That was fine by her. She was happy to sit by him in the Range Rover and talk away to help to relax him. But he wasn't relaxed, she sensed. In fact, he seemed to be becoming moodier by the minute.

The restaurant he had chosen was tiny, just half a dozen tables in a little beamed room. But it was charming, with pretty pink tablecloths and posies of flowers on each table, and though the menu too was small Grant assured her that the food was excellent. She let him choose, and he rapidly ordered antipasto and veal to follow, with a bottle of white wine.

During the meal Grant made more of an effort to talk, but even so, Mandy couldn't keep back a feeling of disappointment. She had expected this to be a

special date. After his half-avowal on the edge of the
broad, she had expected him to behave like a lover
towards her. She was looking for intimacy, and instead
Grant was talking away about the wherries, about
some places in the Broadland that she hadn't yet
visited, about painting. Those were all subjects that
interested them both, but they weren't what she
wanted to hear, and he treated even these neutral subjects in a particularly impersonal way, it seemed to
her, saying almost nothing about his own feelings and
preferences.

'Is there something wrong, Grant?' she asked at
one point, but Grant didn't acknowledge her soft
question, and barely paused in the flow of his conversation. Space-filling, that was what it was, as if he
seemed afraid to let a silence grow between them.

Mandy decided to skip the dessert, though several
of the choices on the menu would have tempted her
at any other time. 'Just coffee,' Grant told the hov-
ering waiter, without bothering to ask her if she
wanted any.

He waited—impatiently, she sensed—for the coffee
to arrive. Mandy took a sip, and then she froze. Grant
was reaching into the pocket of his trousers.

She had no idea what to expect. In fact, he brought
out a folded envelope. He held it in one hand for a
moment, looking down on it with a cold expression,
then he looked across at her and said, 'I got this in
the post this morning.'

'What is it?'

'You'd better look for yourself.'

She took it from him, and turned it over. There was
a New Zealand stamp on it. A hand that somehow

didn't seem to belong to her any more felt inside, and
drew out a sheet of paper headed with the name of
a firm of Auckland solicitors.

She knew what it would contain even before she
read it, but she went doggedly through it, sentence by
sentence. Though the letter was wrapped up in old-
fashioned legal jargon, the meaning was quite clear
to her. Grant had commissioned the solicitors to carry
out an investigation into Frances Blackwater, and they
had come back with a report that showed that Frances
had died in a car crash in 1960. She had died un-
married, only four years after she had emigrated to
Auckland, and long before Mandy herself had been
born.

'Poor Frances,' said Mandy in a low voice.

'Poor Frances,' Grant echoed sardonically. 'How
touching. You almost managed to believe it yourself,
didn't you, that tissue of lies you made up? The lies
about Frances Blackwater, who died young, and never
had a daughter? The lies about you?'

It was funny, she thought, but she almost had.
Frances Blackwater had been a relation of hers, after
all. And even though she knew that the truth was quite
different from the tale she and Dorothy had concocted, and that Frances was a far more distant relation to her than a mother, she felt real sorrow in
seeing this confirmation that the woman she had
known only from a few photographs, the woman who
had looked so much like her, had really died young,
even earlier than Dorothy had imagined.

For a moment her thoughts were quite caught up
with Frances Blackwater and her sad fate, and it didn't
sink in to her what very real danger this letter rep-

resented to her, Mandy Mason. Then she looked up, and saw Grant's cold, accusing face.

At the same time there sank into her the ghastly realisation that she couldn't explain any of her feelings to him. She couldn't tell him how she really felt at this news, couldn't tell him the truth about her relationship to Frances, or to the Blackwaters as a whole. She could only face up in silence to the fact that he knew—knew now, with no room for doubt—that she had lied to him.

'Well?' Grant persisted.

She took a deep breath. 'It's true, Grant. I've known from the start that I wasn't Frances Blackwater's daughter.'

'Then just who the hell are you, Mandy Mason?'

'I can't tell you that. I'm sorry,' she added, lamely.

Grant stared at her. 'Protecting your accomplice?'

She flushed. 'It's nothing like that. But there is a good reason why I can't explain,' she whispered.

'Then tell it to me.'

'I can't do that either.'

'You lying bitch,' Grant hissed. 'And to think I——' His voice faded on a choke, and then he took a breath, and began again, in a colder tone. 'I want you out of Heron's Nest tomorrow.'

Mandy looked down at the pink tablecloth. Out tomorrow! She understood what he was demanding, and why, but there had to be some other way. She had to have time to break this to Dorothy, and to persuade Dorothy to let her tell Grant the truth.

'I can't do that,' she said stubbornly. 'It'll only make Dorothy suspicious.'

'No, it won't. That's what I'm not having, anything that will make Dorothy or James suspect that I've found you out, or even that there was anything to find out. Dorothy couldn't cope with that, and she's not to know.

'I've already worked out how to do it. I've arranged for you to receive a telephone call in the morning, telling you that your "stepmother" has been involved in an accident, and is seriously ill in hospital. You'll pack your bags immediately, and get the three o'clock train from Wroxham. I'll drive you to the station.

'You'll wait three days, then write to Dorothy thanking her for her hospitality. I'll give you six months to tail off your correspondence. Write only when you have to, and make sure that you don't write anything that will make Dorothy suspicious. Then in six months' time you'll write to tell her you're planning to move to a new apartment. You'll send her an address, but a false one. And if she writes to you after that, her letters will be returned marked "address unknown".'

He had it all worked out, Mandy thought to herself. He had considered every last detail. Perhaps he had planned some of it weeks before, when he had first felt that he had cause to suspect her. Then, as soon as the letter had come, he had made the rest of these arrangements, so as to get her quickly and efficiently out of Dorothy's life—and out of his own as well.

'And if I refuse?' she whispered.

'Then I'll show this letter to James in the morning.'

Show it to James. Of course, he wouldn't show it to Dorothy: the whole point of his plan was to protect

Dorothy from unpleasant truths that she wasn't in any state to deal with. Somewhere through the agonised tangle of her emotions it dawned upon Mandy that this threat carried little force. James wouldn't do anything. He'd be shocked and sad, but there was nothing more that either of them could do. Whatever Grant suspected, he didn't have enough evidence to turn to the police.

She thought briefly of facing out his threat, but she couldn't stomach the prospect of James believing that she had lied, and for such base reasons. And even if she did so, she thought, her relationship with Grant had been destroyed beyond redemption, and he would ensure somehow that her friendship with James and Dorothy was destroyed too.

'There's no need for that,' she said. 'I'll do as you suggest.'

'I'm glad you're being sensible,' Grant said grimly. 'Drink your coffee.'

She drank it as rapidly as she could. Grant finished his own coffee just as quickly, and barely ten minutes later they were back in his car. He drove fast, in silence, back to Heron's Nest.

Outside the house, he stopped the car, and paused for a moment before opening the door.

'We're back earlier than they will have expected,' he said curtly. 'Tell them you've a headache, and asked to be brought home.'

She gave a numb nod. The reality of it was only just beginning to sink in. After the following day she would never see Heron's Nest again, never see Dorothy and James, never see Grant again.

That was the worst of it, she thought, turning to him, and seeing his implacable profile facing determinedly away from her. James and Dorothy had liked her and, though they would be disappointed when she dropped out of their lives, she hoped they would continue to think of her with affection. But Grant wouldn't; Grant hated her now.

'Grant,' she began tentatively.

He swung round towards her rapidly, and their eyes connected in a painful flash of recognition. 'Yes?'

'Grant, there is a reason for what I've done. I can't tell it to you, but please believe me, it had absolutely nothing to do with Horace Blackwater or his paintings.'

She expected him to exclaim angrily, leap out and slam the car door against her, but he didn't. Instead he held her gaze for a moment, and then said more gently, 'If only you knew how hard I've tried to believe that there was a different explanation.'

'Then do believe it. Please. I'll do as you say, and leave tomorrow, but I can't bear to go thinking that you hate me.'

'Hate you? Is that what you think?'

In his surprise at her words his guard seemed to have dropped totally, and his face, suddenly open, showed Mandy something very different from hate. Perhaps Grant had been trying to hate her, she realised, but his intense attraction to her had been just as real as hers to him. Even then she could sense it, however hard he had been trying to deny it.

He felt betrayed, she thought suddenly. At least she could understand what he was doing, and why; but he hadn't the remotest understanding of her real motives. In his mind, the lies that she had told had corrupted every single moment of their time together. She thought of the evening they had spent with the photograph albums, and of how Grant must feel now, believing that she had lied as they turned over each page. Even the family tree—he must believe that she had invented the whole thing for his and the Fernhams' benefit, as part of her scheme to defraud them.

She thought too of the evening at Grant's house, when he had told her something about his own family. It had obviously come hard to him to share those facts. How painful he must find it now, thinking as he did that he had shared his feelings with an impostor.

'I'm sorry,' she said again, though she was conscious how hopelessly inadequate the words were to heal his wounds.

Grant's face seemed to close against her. He turned away, then opened the car door. 'Come on,' he said. 'We'll have to be polite to James and Dorothy for five minutes, then I'll go.'

The phone call came in the morning, as Grant had promised. He didn't phone himself; he had obviously realised that Dorothy would answer, and had found a friend to do the job, somebody whose voice Dorothy wouldn't recognise. Mandy listened to his friend reciting the prepared story, and said a few monosyllabic 'yes', 'no' and 'oh's in reply. Then she set down the receiver, and turned to confront Dorothy, who was waiting to hear what it was about.

'Bad news?'

Mandy glanced over Dorothy's shoulder, along the hall to where Mrs Jackson was dusting the banisters.

'Pretty bad,' she said. 'That was a neighbour of my parents'. My stepmother's had an accident, and they've taken her to hospital. I'll have to go down to see her immediately.'

'How terrible!'

'She's not in any danger—it's a broken leg. But all the same, I'll have to go straight away.'

The whole charade unfolded, exactly as Grant had planned it. She had packed most of her things the night before, knowing what was coming, and knowing, too, that she would have to find time to talk to Dorothy. As soon as the wardrobe in the blue room was empty, she went downstairs.

Dorothy was in the conservatory. 'Let me take you out on to the terrace,' said Mandy. 'I want to talk to you before Grant comes.'

It felt so familiar by then, wheeling Dorothy out on to the terrace overlooking the broad. She stopped the wheelchair next to the white-painted table, and sat down beside her mother.

'It shouldn't take more than a day or two, I expect,' Dorothy said in her calm, stubborn voice. 'Just to make sure everything's all right. You'll phone, of course, as soon as you know when you can come back up.'

'I won't be coming back, Dorothy.'

Dorothy turned her head with a speed that Mandy hadn't thought her capable of, and a pair of grey eyes that suddenly bore a startling resemblance to her own fixed hers with great determination.

'But you must come back! You've lots of paintings still to finish, and a contract with the gallery in

Cromer, and quite a few other contacts to follow up, and . . .'

'And we always knew, both of us, right from the start, that I wouldn't be able to stay forever.'

'But the summer! You said all summer . . .'

'Grant knows, Dorothy.'

Dorothy's eyes widened, and then fell in a sudden dejected movement. 'He can't,' she said.

'Not about you. I didn't tell him, I promise. But he does know that I'm not Frances Blackwater's daughter, and that I've lied to James and to him.'

'He can't,' Dorothy whispered again.

'He does. He knows that for certain. Dorothy, if I stay I'll risk hurting you, and James, and my other family back in London too. It's too much. I can't do it. I won't ever be able to come back.'

'But you showed him the photo album, the family tree you'd been working on; we had the story all worked out, and the Blackwater resemblance, and . . .'

And if Dorothy pursued that line of thought, Mandy realised, appalled, she would realise what terrible suspicions Grant was harbouring. 'He saw all those things,' she said quickly. 'And that was the start of it, Dorothy. I realised afterwards that I'd made a couple of stupid mistakes. I muddled up some names and dates: I made your cousin Juliet older than her mother. It was a stupid slip, nothing really to do with our pretence, but Grant picked up on it, and I suppose I panicked a little when he questioned me, and it must have made him suspicious. He brought up the family tree again last night, and kept on and on, asking me questions that I couldn't answer properly. That's when I realised that if I stay any longer there's a danger that he'll uncover the truth. And you don't want that, do you, Dorothy? So now that I have to go back to London in any case, I feel we must face up to the fact that we can't either of us afford for me to come back.'

She tried to keep the cruelty out of her voice, but it was difficult. It was all Dorothy's fault, a little part of her insisted. If Dorothy had only told James the truth, it would never have happened, any of it.

But if Mandy had never wondered about her real mother, she knew, even less would have happened. There were no villains in this story, only fragile human beings who had made mistakes and tried to cover them up, with results that threatened to become disastrous. It wouldn't be a disaster, though, if she left now. She wouldn't let it be a disaster.

'Go down to London for just a week or two,' Dorothy said pleadingly. 'You might feel worried now, but by the time your stepmother's better, Grant will have forgotten all about cousin Juliet. He'll have realised it was just a silly slip, I'm sure. I'm sure he will. There's no possible reason for him to think anything else. You're worrying over nothing, Mandy.'

She wasn't worrying over nothing, and Grant wouldn't forget about it, as Mandy knew only too well. But she didn't dare to insist any more. Dorothy knew as much as it was right for her to know; the rest was her own, to bear as best she could. In time, it would dawn on Dorothy that she really wasn't coming back. She'd made an effort to tell her now; she couldn't do any more.

She got to her feet.

'I've a few more things to pack,' she said. 'You'll call me, Dorothy, when Grant comes for me?'

'I'll call you,' Dorothy agreed brokenly.

She packed. Dorothy called. And Grant came to take her away.

CHAPTER TEN

MANDY'S feet dragged a little as she turned the corner into the road where her flat was situated. It was a long way from the tube, especially when she had a heavy portfolio to carry.

And it seemed even further than it really was, since she had so little to look forward to when she got home. Several of her friends had phoned recently and suggested evenings out, but Mandy never seemed to have the energy to take up their invitations.

She hadn't even done much work since her return to London two weeks previously. She still had a pile of Norfolk watercolours which she was slowly placing in small galleries, and an even larger pile of sketches, but though she didn't mind tramping around the galleries she couldn't face actually working on Broadland scenes. She had phoned a few contacts to see if she could get some other work on commission, but it was high summer and they were all away on holiday. And when she tried to think of different things to paint, her mind seemed to be completely blank. It would only fill with images of Heron's Nest, and of Grant on the *Grey Lady*.

It was pointless, her thinking of those things. She wasn't going to go to Norfolk ever again. She wasn't going to see James and Dorothy ever again. She wasn't going to see Grant again.

Dorothy had phoned once, to see how her stepmother was, and Mandy, temporarily forgetting that she didn't know the accident had been a fabrication, had almost snapped at her instead of answering politely. She herself had written a long, carefully phrased thank-you letter. And then, silence.

Silence which was going to continue, she reminded herself, as she climbed the steps to the flat, propped up her portfolio by the front door and fished for the key. If she wanted her life to be more full, she would have to look in some different direction. Anywhere— except Norfolk.

She opened her bedroom door for just long enough to throw her portfolio down in a corner, then went into the kitchen and made herself a cup of strong black coffee, half-filling the cup with boiling water and topping it up with cold from the tap so that she could drink it quickly. Then she made another, and drank that. Then she looked in the fridge. It was almost empty, and none too clean, but she found a hunk of pâté, and a length of rather stale French bread in the breadbin, and sat down at the table to eat them. She didn't even bother with a plate.

She made a third cup of coffee and went into her bed-sitting-room. She switched the television on, and watched the first thing that appeared, without bothering to check out the other channels—a cricket match. It was life after a fashion. She knew nothing about cricket; she had no idea which teams were playing.

The doorbell rang, faintly over the sound of the television. She got up slowly. She wasn't expecting any callers, but she thought it might be her friend Geraldine, or one of the people from the other flats in the block wanting to borrow some sugar or half a pint of milk.

She opened the door without bothering with the security chain, and stared blankly at the tall figure confronting her. It couldn't really be Grant. It couldn't possibly be Grant. She turned away, half thinking that the apparition that couldn't really be Grant would disappear when she stopped looking at it.

'Mandy,' Grant said, in a curiously tentative voice.

She took a few steps, then stopped half-way down the hallway. Something strange was stirring in the deadened layers of her mind. That wasn't fair. It didn't hurt quite unbearably so long as she felt deadened. But this was unbearable, this stirring, this seeing and hearing a person who surely couldn't be Grant. She had been trying to pretend that Grant Livingstone didn't exist, not anywhere in the world, and here he was, in front of her. He couldn't be.

Here he was, taking her in his arms, while her mind numbly insisted that this couldn't happen. Here he was, crushing her to him and murmuring her name, over and over. Then his mouth groped for hers, and found it, and Mandy's heart awoke like the Sleeping Beauty's, and she knew that she was alive again, and he was real after all.

She was feeling fully alive—rather more than just alive, in fact—by the time he gently released her. He kept his hands round her waist, as if he was afraid she would stumble without his sustaining support. He looked her over critically.

'You've got thinner,' he said. 'You haven't been eating properly.'

'So've you,' she retorted, taking in for the first time the dark shadows under his eyes. 'And what are you—why are you——' Her mind was whirling. She sensed that something had happened to bring him to London. Things had changed between them, he was on her side again now—but what had changed his attitude, and how?

'I had to come and sort things out,' Grant said. 'Is there somewhere we can go? Somewhere to sit down?'

'In here,' she said dazedly, leading him into her room. The cricket was still plodding away on the television. Grant released her hand for just long enough to turn it off, then came back to her, and drew her to sit next to him on her bed.

For a moment Mandy couldn't bring herself to talk, and Grant didn't seem to want to speak either. Just to know that he was there, in London, and that she could look at him and touch him and be with him, was more than enough.

He held her for a long time, in a tight hug, then he loosed his grip, and nudged her chin upwards with a gentle finger, so that her eyes connected with his.

'You know,' she said wonderingly.

'I think I do,' Grant agreed. 'At least, I know a lot of it, much more than I did two weeks ago. That's why I came, to tell you that I understand now. But there are still some gaps missing. I think I understand, but I'm not absolutely certain that I've got it right. You're the only person who can fill them in for me.'

'I can't,' she whispered.

'I think perhaps you'll find that you can. They're only little gaps. You'll be confirming what I've guessed, rather than giving away a secret. Let me tell you what I already know.'

He tightened the arm that he had round her, drawing her close and encouraging her to settle her head against his broad shoulder, as he began to explain to her how he had learned much of the truth. He had, she now discovered, set in motion two different lines of enquiry when he had first learned that Dorothy had invited Mandy to stay at Heron's Nest. He had enquired about Frances Blackwater in New Zealand, and he had enquired about Mandy Mason in London.

'The New Zealanders replied very rapidly,' he explained, 'but at first the enquiry service I used in England came up with a blank. There were several Amanda Jean Masons whose births were registered at about the right time. I told them to check all of them out, but it was soon apparent that none of them was you. I almost gave up then, thinking that you might have used a totally false name, but I asked them what other lines of enquiry they generally took, and then they gave me the idea that you might have been adopted.'

'So they found me.'

'That's right. Baby daughter Amanda Jean, adopted by Albert and Elizabeth Mason. Of course there's a record in existence of your name at birth, and of your mother's name but that's private. You yourself can ask to have access to it, but it's not open to curious members of the public like me.'

She knew all this. It had taken her months to find out her real parentage, and she remembered vividly what care the authorities had taken before allowing her to see the original entry that had been made before her adoption. Grant obviously wouldn't have been able to see it.

'So you still don't know who my real parents were,' she said slowly. Had he guessed? she wondered. Did he really know so much that it would be no betrayal for her to tell him the rest, or was Dorothy's secret still secure?

'Not for certain. But when I tried to think what other reason you might have had for coming to Heron's Nest, there was only one answer that made any sense. I told the enquiry service to see if they could come up with anything for Blackwater, and yesterday they came back to me with the information. Baby daughter Susannah, born to Dorothy Mary Blackwater, father unknown.'

He knew it all, then; or at least, all of it that mattered.

'Wait here a minute,' she said.

She went over to her desk in the corner, and rummaged through a crowded drawer full of papers. The papers she needed weren't in her family-tree folder: they were ones she had taken out of it when she was pretending to be Frances's daughter.

Finally she located them, and with quiet triumph she handed them over to Grant.

He looked carefully at them all: the adoption certificate, the photocopy of her application to see her original birth certificate, and the certificate itself with its covering letter.

Last of all he turned back to the application. His eyes lingered, she saw, on the date.

'February this year.'

'That's right,' she said. It was such a relief to talk about it to someone: she had never before told anyone the full story. 'I'd been thinking of doing it for as long as I can remember, but I had to wait until I was old enough, and then I had second thoughts about it and didn't apply right away. It wasn't till late last year that I finally sent off to see my records. I had to go through a counselling process—they warn you that your mother might not want to know you, and give you some advice on how to approach her if you're determined to. They're ever so slow, too. First I had to get my birth certificate, then I had to find out Dorothy Blackwater's married name, and then I had to check on her address. That took me until April.'

'And in May you came to Heron's Nest.'

She nodded. 'By then I was really desperate to find out more. I wanted so much to know what Dorothy looked like, where she lived, what kind of a person she was—oh, everything!'

'Of course you would,' Grant agreed gravely.

'But I was scared, too. They really rub it in at the counselling sessions that it's terribly easy to muck up your mother's life if you approach her in the wrong way. You have to break it to her gently who you are, and you have to make sure that you don't let anyone else know what you're up to. Lots of women keep it secret that they've had a baby adopted, apparently, even from their parents or their husbands. The counsellors don't tell you what to do, mind—just what not to do! If you make a phone call, someone else might overhear; if you write a letter, then someone else might read it.'

'So you decided to come up in person.'

Mandy nodded. 'I wasn't sure what exactly to do when I got there, so I thought I'd play it by ear. I'd come to Little Catwood and look around, and perhaps ask a few questions. The barmaid in the pub told me the way to Heron's Nest, and she warned me that Dorothy wouldn't be there. I thought I'd sneak a look at the house, and then I couldn't resist writing a note to Dorothy, saying just enough to pave the way, so that she might realise right away who I was when I phoned her. *If* I'd ever dared to phone her!'

'At least you did that,' Grant said with a smile.

'Actually I didn't. You scared me away.' She went on to explain about the phone call Dorothy herself had made, and about the story that they had invented between them, to enable Mandy to return to Heron's Nest without anyone else knowing who she really was.

'You should have insisted that she told James,' Grant said sternly. 'I can understand that she would have found it hard, but she really should have told him.'

'I hoped she would,' she said fervently. 'All along I've hoped she would, Grant. But she won't. She'll never tell him.'

'Never's a long time.'

'Yes,' agreed Mandy doubtfully. 'It is. And I'd so much like to be proved wrong. But we mustn't assume that she'll decide to tell him just because we want her to.'

'I'm not assuming it because of that, I'm assuming it because it's the right and only thing to do. Dorothy's a brave woman, and she'll see that, I'm sure. I'll talk to her about it when I get back home.'

It was touching, Grant's confidence in his ability to persuade Dorothy—and convincing, too. If anyone could talk her round, thought Mandy, then Grant would be able to. And now that Grant himself knew her secret there was even less excuse for her to keep it from James. Mandy thought there was a chance he might be right, and she so much hoped that he would be.

'Still,' she said quietly, 'the important thing is that we've no secrets between the two of us now.'

'Nothing else? No other lies at all?'

'No big ones, I promise you.'

'Little ones, you mean? Come on, spill the beans! Confess everything!'

'Well,' she managed to say—with difficulty, because Grant was tickling her to make her confess, 'I did invent a holiday to try and fool you...'

She never finished explaining about the holiday, because Grant suddenly seemed to have lost interest in hearing her confessions. He swept the mass of papers off the bed, and pushed her backwards against the pillows, covering her with his long body, and finding her mouth again with his.

He released her lips for long enough to whisper 'Forgive me,' and Mandy managed to say 'Of course,' before he claimed them again. Then she was lost in the sheer heat and force and passion of his lovemaking.

Nothing could have stopped them now. Tension and guilt and confusion had held them back for so many weeks, and now that the air was cleared it seemed that there was an irresistible force urging them to join their bodies together. Grant's hands moved over her, firm, confident, pulling off her clothing and throwing it aside with sublime indifference to where it ended up. Within minutes she was naked, and everywhere they touched she burned with desire for him.

She had thought it would be awkward, embarrassing, making love to a man fully for the first time, but in fact the urgency swept all the awkwardness away, and she was only impatient to enjoy more of him, and more. When Grant reached down to fumble with the fastening of his denims, she brought her own hands to help him. He shrugged his trousers off impatiently, moved back on top of her, and then he was in her, and his body was arrogantly asserting its possession of hers.

She had never dreamed of anything so elemental, so irresistible, so utterly glorious. A rhythm as powerful and implacable as the surge of the sea seemed to be sweeping through her with every thrust of his powerful male body. The waves mounted higher and higher, filling and fulfilling her, and yet awakening in her a greater and greater longing. She hovered for a moment on an unbearable peak of ecstasy. Then it was as if it had exploded within her, and she had soared into a mindless expanse where nothing existed but the basic reality of their two bodies mingled into one.

She floated there for a seeming eternity. Then slowly, slowly, she found herself coming back to earth: to the reality, solid, sweaty, but none the less glorious, of herself and Grant, stretched out across a bed which had never witnessed such scenes of abandonment before.

Slowly her eyes and Grant's adjusted their focus, and from the contemplation of the infinite they came back to earth to centre on each other.

'That was your first time,' he said in awed amazement.

'So it was,' she agreed.

'I was horribly impatient.'

'I thought it was wonderful.'

'Yes, it was.' He smiled. 'My love.'

The second time was slower, much slower, and after that they slept. Mandy woke to a warm morning, and to the light of a clear summer day streaming through the curtains she had never got around to closing the night before.

She lay for a moment, silently watching Grant sleeping by her side. He *was* thinner than he had been in Norfolk. He had lost sleep over her, she thought with a kind of shocked delight, but now he seemed completely at peace. And she felt strangely relaxed, and yet somehow glowing: at ease in her body, and at the same time more aware of it than she had ever been before.

She went and showered, peeped in again to see that Grant still had not stirred, and went to the kitchen to make coffee. He appeared just as she was sitting down to drink it, wearing his denims and nothing else, and looking large and male and still extremely sleepy.

'Got any more of that?' he asked, peering absently into her cup.

'I reckon I can find another one,' she laughed, getting up to make him some. He came up behind her

and put his arms round her, and she turned to reach
up and give him a long, lingering kiss.

'I'll have to get back to Wroxham today,' he said,
after the first few sips of coffee had restored him to
something like normal functioning. 'And I can't see
that I'll be able to come down here again, not for a
while at least. We've still got every boat out, and
James wouldn't be able to manage without me. But
you can come up to Heron's Nest, can't you? And
stay with Dorothy and James until we plan out when
we're going to get married and everything?'

She stared open-mouthed at him.

'I can't see how I can,' she said at last. 'Not until—
not *unless*—Dorothy brings herself to tell James the
truth.'

'She will,' Grant said confidently. 'She's got to, now
that I know it. I'm sure she'll see that. Anyway, she
won't get you back until she tells him, and she wants
you to come back, doesn't she?'

'What she wants is for me to come back and keep
on lying, Grant. And I can't.'

'I'll talk to her,' Grant said. 'Don't worry about it.
I'm sure it'll all work out. Now, how about some
breakfast? And then I'll have to be on my way.'

The night had made him hungry, she thought, with
an inward smile at the obviousness of the male animal.
Then she discovered it had made her hungry, too, and
her teasing faded. Her fridge was no better equipped
than it had been the night before, so she had to dash
down to the corner shop to replenish her supplies. By
the time she returned Grant had made more coffee,
and between them they devoured almost an entire loaf
of bread and six eggs.

It was the happiest meal she had ever known, full
of laughter and loving looks. Happiness seemed to
fill her so full that there simply wasn't any room for
fear that Grant might be wrong. But then he gathered
up his things, kissed her one last time, and strode off
towards the tube station, and Mandy was left with an
empty flat, and with a cold, hollow terror that
Dorothy would never bring herself to do it.

Grant phoned that evening, to tell her that he loved
and missed her. Mandy told him a great deal on the
same lines in return. He didn't mention Dorothy or
James, though, and she assumed that he hadn't yet
had a chance to speak to Dorothy, and had nothing
to report.

He phoned again the next evening, but again there
was no mention of Dorothy. On the third evening she
brought herself to ask him what was happening.

'I reckon it's going to take time,' Grant said.

His voice was gentle over the phone, deliberately
reassuring. But under the gentleness, she sensed his
anger and frustration. He had thought it would be
easy, she thought to herself, and now he knew that it
wasn't going to be easy at all.

She tried to stay hopeful throughout the next week,
and the next. Grant phoned often, and wrote to her
too—long, loving letters full of warm words and
private jokes, but conspicuously short of mentions of
Dorothy and James. How long? Mandy couldn't help
asking herself, as she read them. How long?

Ten days after he had left her, he phoned and said,
'I'll come down to see you this weekend, if you'll let
me.'

'Let you?'

'Just checking. I'll be working late on Friday, so I'll drive down on Saturday morning, and be with you at about eleven. OK?'

'Wonderful,' she assured him.

It *would* be wonderful to see him, she thought, as she put the receiver down. But it was worrying, too. She sensed that he wasn't coming with any good news about Dorothy, and without Dorothy's co-operation she couldn't see how their relationship could ever progress any further. She couldn't conceivably plan to marry Grant while James didn't know the truth about her background. It was a lie that affected not only her and Dorothy, but Bert and Beth Mason and all her other relatives, too.

She worked hard for the rest of the week, since she was still trying to make up for the fallow period after she had come back from Norfolk, and was still working up till the time Grant appeared on Saturday.

'I'll just put all my stuff away,' she said after greeting him, leaving him to follow her into her bed-sitting-room.

He came up to her drawing-board, and peered over her shoulder at the wet painting that was pinned on it. 'You're still working on the Norfolk stuff?'

'That's right. I've enough material to last me for several weeks more, and I'm really enjoying working on it. It's just the right kind of scenery to suit my style. I feel now as if I've found my niche as an artist. Dorothy thought the opposite, funnily enough—that seeing Horace Blackwater's work would cramp my style, but it hasn't, not at all.'

He gazed at the sketch pinned on her board for a moment, and Mandy, giving up her attempt to clear everything away, watched him. She couldn't make out his expression. There was something to it, something that wasn't exactly sad, but wasn't relaxed and cheerful either.

'Ever been to the Caribbean?' he said quite suddenly, looking up at her.

'The Caribbean? No, of course not. Why, have you?'

'A couple of times, yes. I crewed yachts there when I was a teenager.'

'That's nice,' she said, sitting down on her bed and feeling totally confused.

'You think you'd like it, then?'

'Like it? But, Grant, I...we...'

'We'll have to get away from Norfolk,' Grant said brusquely. 'For a while, at least. I thought maybe the Caribbean would suit us.' She opened her mouth to protest, but he went on determinedly, cutting her off before she could speak, 'It's not what you were thinking of, I know, but I reckon we could make it work. The money I'd get for my share of Catwood Wherrymen would buy us a decent yacht. We'd sail it over to Bermuda or somewhere, and then charter it out, acting as crew. It's a good life. I know quite a few people who've done it.'

'But, Grant, that's——'

'I'd make sure you had some chances to paint,' Grant persisted. 'The scenery's nothing like Norfolk, but you're a versatile artist, and I hope you'd find a way to handle it. It wouldn't be forever, of course. When we really wanted to settle down, we'd most

likely come back to England again. The Thames barge
business might suit me; it isn't so very different from
wherries.'

'But you *are* settled down!' she spluttered. 'Grant,
you belong in Norfolk!'

Grant silently shook his head. 'I've thought hard
about it, Mandy, very hard. That's what I've thought
for years, that I belong in Norfolk, but now I reckon
the answer's different. I belong with you.'

'But the yard, the boats . . .'

'That wouldn't be a problem. We've had a very
good summer so far, and the business is in good shape.
Early autumn's the perfect time to sell. I doubt if
James would want to take over my share, but I know
a couple of men who would be interested to go in with
him. By November or the latest it should all be fixed,
and then we can get married and set off for the sun.'

He smiled as he said this, and tried to meet her eye,
but she wasn't in any state to respond. His suggestion
had shaken her to the core.

Grant would do this for me! she thought in
amazement. He'd leave Norfolk, leave his yard and
his beloved wherries, leave all his friends, so that he
can marry me! She could have asked for no greater
proof of his feelings for her.

It filled her with joy to know that Grant loved her
enough to suggest such a thing, but at the same time,
she knew that she couldn't let him do it. It wasn't
right. Grant *did* belong in Norfolk. Maybe he had
enjoyed the Caribbean as a boy; maybe he would
enjoy it now, if they were to go there for a wonderful
holiday. But he wasn't suggesting taking a holiday in
the Caribbean, he was suggesting making their home

there. The West Indies weren't his home, and she couldn't see how they ever could be. They were too different from Norfolk. He had no roots there, no friends. Norfolk was his home, and he needed that home.

She couldn't help thinking of the evening when he had stretched out on the hearthrug at his house, and told her of his family, with such bleakness in his voice. He had worked hard to grow roots for himself to make up for the ones that his childhood hadn't given him. He had found a place, a job, people with whom he belonged. He had a great sense of security, but it had taken him years to build that up, and now he talked of throwing it all away!

Perhaps he thought she didn't understand that, Mandy thought to herself. But she did. She had thought she had found a home in Norfolk too, and then after only a few short weeks she had lost it again. Make Grant lose *his* home, too? And after not weeks, but years in which the Broads had worked their quiet spell on him? No, she couldn't do that to him!

'No, Grant,' she said in a quiet but steady voice.

'It's the only way, Mandy. Don't you see? I've tried to persuade Dorothy, but I know now that it'll take her years to come round, if she ever does. We can't marry and live in Norfolk, not while James doesn't know the truth. But this way we *could* marry, without hurting anyone else. I'm sure I could make James believe that this is what we really want to do. He'll have no reason at all to suspect the truth. We could still stay in touch with the Fernhams, but we wouldn't have to see them regularly and keep living a lie.'

Without hurting anyone? But it would hurt you, Grant, she thought silently. It would hurt me. And it would hurt Dorothy and James too, to lose us both.

'No, Grant,' she repeated. 'It's a wonderful offer, but the answer's no.'

'Thank about it, Mandy, please. Don't dismiss the idea just like that. I know it's not what you expected, but that doesn't mean it couldn't work. Take some time to get used to the idea before you decide.'

She shook her head. She couldn't bear to think about it. She couldn't afford to think about it. The only way she would ever survive the end of her relationship with Grant was to do it quickly, she thought. Torment herself by playing with this crazy idea of his, when all the time she knew that it would be wrong, wrong, wrong to agree to it? A thousand times no.

'Grant, I think you'd better leave.'

She thought for a moment that he would take her in his arms, and try to persuade her that way. If he had, she knew that she couldn't possibly have resisted him. But he didn't. He stood there for a moment, leaning against her drawing-board with its pictures of Catwood Broad, and looking steadily across the room at her. Then he walked across and kissed her, very gently, on the forehead. Then, without speaking any more, he turned and left her.

CHAPTER ELEVEN

'HELLO, Mandy, it's James Fernham,' said the voice over the telephone.

'Oh. Hello, James.'

She was so amazed that James should call that she hardly knew what to say. It was more than a month since she had last seen Grant, seven weeks since she had left Heron's Nest, and apart from a couple of phone calls from Dorothy to make sure that her stepmother was recovering well she had heard nothing from either of the Fernhams in all that time.

'Mandy, there's something I need to talk to you about. I'll be down in London on Thursday. Could we possibly meet then? For lunch, perhaps?'

She hesitated. 'I've a temporary job at the moment, James. Clerking, not far from Oxford Circus. I'll only have an hour for lunch, from one to two.'

'That should be long enough.'

They agreed to meet in a pub just off Carnaby Street. It wasn't the ideal location, but Mandy couldn't think of anywhere else that was likely to be reasonably quiet on a Thursday lunchtime.

James hadn't given any indication why he had called, she thought, as she put the phone down. It was probably something purely practical. A query from a Norfolk gallery owner, perhaps, or even a chance to return something she had left behind at

Heron's Nest. She mustn't let herself think that it would change things.

She wished he hadn't called, wished she didn't have to see him. Not that she didn't like James—she did, very much—but she didn't want any more reminders about Grant, not when she was working hard on forgetting him. That had been proving difficult enough as it was. It would be even harder if James told her all about what he was doing and how he was feeling.

She slept badly that night, and woke up when her alarm went off with a dream fresh in her head. She and Grant had been alone on the Broads, sailing the *Grey Lady* together, the vast black sail flapping gently above their heads, the sun shining on the water. Just a phone call from James, she thought ruefully, and Grant had reclaimed her thoughts as totally as if he had never left them. He never really had.

Fortunately she was busy that morning. It was the second week of her current temporary job: a dull one, consisting mainly of addressing envelopes, copying the names and addresses from endless lists. She worked so hard, and so blankly, that it was a surprise to realise, at one o'clock, that she had done twice as many of the envelopes as usual.

James Fernham was waiting in the pub when she reached it, drinking a pint of beer and looking acutely ill at ease in his business suit.

'I'm hardly ever down in London,' he explained, as they made their way to a relatively quiet corner of the bar. 'Grant usually comes down where there's business to see to. But we thought it would be best if I talked to you about this first.'

'There's nothing wrong with Dorothy?' she asked, suddenly apprehensive. 'Or Grant?'

'No, they're fine.' James hesitated. 'Well, not fine, exactly. They've been missing you badly. We've all missed you.'

'I've missed you too,' said Mandy. 'But I had a lot of things to see to in London, James. I really couldn't have come back up to Norfolk, even after my stepmother was out of hospital.'

'You don't have to lie to me, Mandy. I know all about it now.'

'All about . . .'

'Everything. I hope.'

James cast a sideways look at her, and then looked away. He was obviously acutely embarrassed. He did, she thought suddenly; he knew it all.

'Dorothy told you,' she said.

James gave an awkward nod. 'I'm sorry, Mandy,' he said with sudden vehemence. 'It's not that I'm annoyed at you, it's not your fault. But it's not easy to take, something like this. I thought I knew Dorothy so well, and to find out that she'd kept it from me, all these years . . . I didn't know I could be so angry.' He turned to her, and met her eyes, with his anguish clear on his face. 'It's the first time I've ever shouted at her.'

'A lot of men would have done more than shout,' she said gently.

'But I'm not a lot of men. I'm Dorothy's husband. And I——' James looked away abruptly. His shoulders shook convulsively, and he took a hefty gulp of his beer to hide his emotion. 'Anyway,' he went on, a moment later, 'now I know.'

'I'm sorry,' she whispered.

'You don't have to be sorry,' James said sharply. 'You just have to come back.'

'James, that's so kind of you, but I can't come back, not yet. Not until—not *unless* you're happy with the idea. You have to take some time to get used to it. Now that you know, there's no need to rush things.'

'You have to come back,' James persisted. 'Grant's been like a shadow since you left. And Dorothy needs you.'

'But you, James...'

'I want you back, too.' James's hand clenched around his glass. 'This is harder than I expected. It's more than a week since Dorothy told me, and I thought, I can't leave it any longer, I've got to get it over with, but I don't know how to——' He looked around wildly, and found a table where he deposited his glass. 'I'll just have to go for a walk,' he muttered to her, and pushed his way out of the bar.

She waited until five to two, but he didn't come back again.

She went back to work in a daze. Poor James, she kept thinking. To discover something like that, out of the blue. She thought, too, of Dorothy, plucking up all her courage and telling him; and of Grant, like a shadow since she left, thinking that there was no hope.

And now there was hope, of a sort. A part of her was aching to rush to Liverpool Street station and buy a ticket for the first train to Norfolk. But, inside, she knew that she had been right to urge James to take the time to get used to the new situation. She hoped and hoped that he would manage to, but she didn't dare to take advantage of his generosity, and push him too hard.

She had been planning to go out that evening with a group of friends, but she made an excuse and stayed in by the telephone. She was sure one of them would ring, but she wasn't sure which of them it would be.

It was Grant.

'James is terribly upset,' she burst out.

Grant's voice, crackling slightly on the line, sounded calm and reassuring and safe. 'Of course he is,' he said. 'But he's over the worst, Mandy. He was wound up like a watchspring at the thought of going down to London and telling you. Now he's unwound. But he's also pretty exhausted, with relief, and annoyance because he feels he made a mess of it, and worry because he doesn't know what you're going to do next.'

'Nothing, darling. How can I?'

'No, you have to come back. Even if it's only for a day or two at first, just to show them both that it's going to be all right.'

'But Grant...' She was going to insist that she couldn't, but she suddenly changed her mind. 'Grant, is Dorothy all right? All the strain of this, is she...'

'She hasn't had a relapse, if that's what you're afraid of. She was very low after you left, though, Mandy. I know she's not a very motherly person, and she found it hard to know how to treat you, but it did matter enormously to her to have you back in her life, and I think she really was devastated at the thought that she had lost you again.'

'And then you told her that you knew, and...'

'I did it gently, honestly I did, and at the time she was so hostile that I really felt there was no hope of her agreeing to tell James. But she must have mulled over it afterwards, and when she realised that I too had lost you because of her decision, she plucked up her courage. I didn't keep pressing her, Mandy. It was her choice to tell him, and she made the decision all by herself.'

'How wonderful of her,' said Mandy sincerely.

'She's a brave woman, I told you that. No saint, but a very determined and courageous lady all the same. I think she's relieved, in a way, that James too has proved to be clay-footed. It's been good for them both, that he's been angry enough not to try and hide it.'

'He's such a good man, Grant.'

'He is,' Grant said firmly. 'And he'll come to accept it, and to treat you like a daughter. So long as you don't expect——'

'I don't expect a fairy-tale ending,' she assured him. 'I don't expect everything to be wonderful overnight, and I don't imagine that it will be easy for any of us. But if I can only keep a little place in both their lives...'

'And a big place in mine,' Grant finished for her. 'Come up this weekend, Mandy. Just to talk it over, and to reassure Dorothy.'

'OK,' she agreed. 'I'll see you on Saturday.'

The rickety little train pulled painfully slowly into Wroxham. Past the back gardens, over the river, and into the station. Mandy grabbed her bag from the luggage rack and was out of the door almost before the train had come to a halt.

Grant was there, on the platform. She stood there for a moment, just looking at him, looking tall and tanned and incredibly happy. And then they were hurtling down the platform towards each other, and his strong arms were round her, and he was picking her up and swinging her in the air from sheer joy.

'Welcome home,' he whispered, when he had set her down again.

She looked up at him. The world was whirling dizzily around her, and there was Grant, the still centre of it, holding her safe.

'It's not home yet,' she teased him.

'But it soon will be,' he said firmly. His eyes met hers, the sun catching the flecks of gold in them, and his mouth just touched hers, carrying with it a thousand promises of the love they would share.

It was almost dark when Grant's Range Rover pulled up outside the gates that marked the entrance to Catwood Wherrymen. They were locked, and he had to get out and unlock them before driving in and parking on the forecourt.

'This way,' he said.

Holding hands, he and Mandy made their way past the offices, along the riverbank, past the boatsheds, and towards the cutting where the wherries were moored.

It was mid-September, towards the very end of the holiday season, and three of the wherries lay end to end along the quay, their heavy sails lowered. Mandy and Grant walked past two of them, and stopped at the third. In the half-light they could just read the nameplate on the cabin side: *Grey Lady*.

Grant stepped on first, and then helped her to clamber aboard. He led the way along the plankway to the double doors that opened into the wherry-master's cabin, opened them, and went inside. The wherry had just been cleaned after its return from a week's cruising: the two bunks were neatly made, and the stove shone black at the far end of the narrow space between them.

Mandy followed him in, and turned to close the doors behind them. It was very quiet in the cabin. They could just hear the splash of water against the wherry's sides, and the faint sounds of talk and laughter from the riverside pubs.

'We could take her out tomorrow,' Grant said thoughtfully.

'Could we manage her together?'

'I think so. I know you've no experience, but I could tell you just what to do. You're strong enough to act as mate, and the river isn't crowded at this time of year. And there's something to be said for staying away from Heron's Nest for most of the day.'

There was. Dorothy and James had both been welcoming, but they were both edgy, and Mandy knew the weekend would be easier if she saw them only for short stretches.

'I suppose,' she said, sitting down on one of the narrow bunks, 'I'll never really be a part of their family.'

Grant came to sit next to her. 'If you want a new family,' he said softly, 'then we'll make one together.'

'Sounds good,' she agreed.

She meant it with all her heart. That was how it would be, she thought, and how it ought to be. She had left her home with Beth and Bert because it was time for her to grow up. She needed to make a new home for herself, but it wasn't going to be with Dorothy and James. Dorothy had already given her what she had most needed from her: a knowledge of the place where she belonged and the people she belonged to, and the confidence that came with that knowledge. And now, on the basis of her new-found self-confidence and her new happiness, she could start to build her own life with the man she loved.

Dorothy would have a place in it always, she hoped, and James too, but they could never be a conventional mother and father to her. She suspected that they were both realistic enough to know that, and that soon they would break to her the news that they wanted her to keep on appearing to the rest of the world as their distant relative, Frances Blackwater's daughter. That thought didn't give her any pain, because now she knew not only who she really was, but who she was going to be. Mrs Grant Livingstone. That would be her family now: her and Grant, and perhaps one day the children they would have together.

'Let's do that,' she whispered.

Grant's kiss this time didn't just hold a promise, it held a commitment. That this was her home, this her man, this where she belonged: with Grant, in his house, his boat, his world.

It was warm in the little cabin, with the two of them squashed together on the bunk. Grant undressed her slowly and unhurriedly, and she undressed him. The flickering light from the cabin's one lamp brought red glints from his hair, and shone reflected in his eyes.

She ran her hands over the firm, muscular flesh of his shoulders and upper arms, full of wonder at the strength and beauty of him.

Though the bunk was barely wide enough for Mandy herself to lie flat, there was room for Grant to bend over her, and to claim possession of her body with his hands and his mouth. His tongue lazily explored the lower slopes of her breasts, and his teeth gently nipped at the rosy peak. His mouth traced paths of awareness down the faint swell of her stomach, and just skimmed the delicate flesh of her inner thighs. She trembled, and curved her body upwards to meet his touch.

'No hurry,' Grant's voice whispered, though the firm touch of his hands, the feel of his thighs, strong and muscular as she wrapped her legs around his, the faint shudder of his body as she ran her fingernails down his spine, all told her that every moment of delay was sweet agony to both of them.

He caressed her for a long, long time, with all the sensuous patience that she had first seen when he was working with his boats. Her body glowed with desire, her mind was overflowing with joy in the knowledge of his love for her, and hers for him.

Then they could wait no longer, and he was driving into her, and each strong thrust of his body brought new waves of delight pulsing through hers. His rhythm quickened, and the bud of taut longing inside Mandy broke into a flower of fire, its petals spreading, its warmth licking through every limb. She heard Grant exclaim in exultant wonder, his body fusing with hers in the intensity of their delight. And then he was collapsing against her, his breath even shorter and more ragged than hers, the weight of him solid and comforting as her body slowly relaxed into a sleepy fulfilment.

In the stillness of the aftermath, the timbers of the *Grey Lady* creaked very gently, as if they too were relaxing with warm satisfaction, and the big boat rocked almost imperceptibly on the quiet water of the river.

They lay there for some time, barely moving, listening to the regular thud of each other's heartbeat and the slowly easing rhythm of each other's breath. Then Grant moved, cautiously, easing his weight off the narrow bunk.

'The next time I build a wherry,' he said softly, 'I reckon I'll say to hell with tradition, and put a double bunk in the master's cabin.'

Mandy shook her head. 'No, I wouldn't have a new boat. I want this one to be ours, our special boat. I want us to sail her together, just the two of us.'

'Only in the autumn and spring, my dear,' Grant laughed. 'I've a living to make, and this lovely lady needs to earn her keep. But we'll sail her right across the Broadland together, from Horsey Mere to Breydon Water. And you shall sketch every turn in the river, every corner of every broad as we go. There are a million different sights to be seen from a wherry, and I want you to capture them all.'

Mandy smiled. 'Even Horace Blackwater only managed a few thousand, darling.'

'You can stop at half a dozen, if you like. Whatever makes you happy.'

'I already know what makes me happy,' she murmured, her eyes on Grant's tall shape, so oddly at home in the tiny cabin. 'You do.'

Harlequin Presents

Coming Next Month

Available in September wherever paperback books are sold, or through Harlequin Reader Service:

In the U.S.
901 Fuhrmann Blvd.
P.O. Box 1397
Buffalo, N.Y. 14240-1397

In Canada
P.O. Box 603
Fort Erie, Ontario
L2A 5X3

HARLEQUIN'S WISHBOOK
SWEEPSTAKES RULES & REGULATIONS
NO PURCHASE NECESSARY TO ENTER OR RECEIVE A PRIZE

1. To enter and join the Reader Service, affix the Four Free Books and Free Gifts sticker along with both of your other Sweepstakes stickers to the Sweepstakes Entry Form. If you do not wish to take advantage of our Reader Service, but wish to enter the Sweepstakes only, do not affix the Four Free Books and Free Gifts sticker to the Sweepstakes Entry Form. Incomplete and/or inaccurate entries are ineligible for that section or sections of prizes. Not responsible for mutilated or unreadable entries or inadvertent printing errors. Mechanically reproduced entries are null and void.

2. Whether you take advantage of this offer or not, your Sweepstakes numbers will be compared against a list of winning numbers generated at random by the computer. In the event that all prizes are not claimed by March 31, 1992, a random drawing will be held from all qualified entries received from March 30, 1990 to March 31, 1992, to award all unclaimed prizes. All cash prizes (Grand to Sixth), will be mailed to the winners and are payable by check in U.S. funds. Seventh prize to be shipped to winners via third-class mail. These prizes are in addition to any free, surprise or mystery gifts that might be offered. Versions of this sweepstakes with different prizes of approximate equal value may appear in other mailings or at retail outlets by Torstar Corp. and its affiliates.

3. The following prizes are awarded in this sweepstakes: ★ Grand Prize (1) $1,000,000; First Prize (1) $25,000; Second Prize (1) $10,000; Third Prize (5) $5,000; Fourth Prize (10) $1,000; Fifth Prize (100) $250; Sixth Prize (2500) $10; ★ ★ Seventh Prize (6000) $12.95 ARV.

   ★ This Sweepstakes contains a Grand Prize offering of $1,000,000 annuity. Winner will receive $33,333.33 a year for 30 years without interest totalling $1,000,000.

   ★ ★ Seventh Prize: A fully illustrated hardcover book published by Torstar Corp. Approximate value of the book is $12.95.

   Entrants may cancel the Reader Service at any time without cost or obligation to buy (see details in center insert card).

4. This promotion is being conducted under the supervision of Marden-Kane, Inc., an independent judging organization. By entering this Sweepstakes, each entrant accepts and agrees to be bound by these rules and the decisions of the judges, which shall be final and binding. Odds of winning in the random drawing are dependent upon the total number of entries received. Taxes, if any, are the sole responsibility of the winners. Prizes are nontransferable. All entries must be received by no later than 12:00 NOON, on March 31, 1992. The drawing for all unclaimed sweepstakes prizes will take place May 30, 1992, at 12:00 NOON, at the offices of Marden-Kane, Inc., Lake Success, New York.

5. This offer is open to residents of the U.S., the United Kingdom, France and Canada, 18 years or older except employees and their immediate family members of Torstar Corp., its affiliates, subsidiaries, Marden-Kane, Inc., and all other agencies and persons connected with conducting this Sweepstakes. All Federal, State and local laws apply. Void wherever prohibited or restricted by law. Any litigation respecting the conduct and awarding of a prize in this publicity contest may be submitted to the Régie des loteries et courses du Québec.

6. Winners will be notified by mail and may be required to execute an affidavit of eligibility and release which must be returned within 14 days after notification or an alternative winner will be selected. Canadian winners will be required to correctly answer an arithmetical skill-testing question administered by mail which must be returned within a limited time. Winners consent to the use of their names, photographs and/or likenesses for advertising and publicity in conjunction with this and similar promotions without additional compensation.

7. For a list of our major winners, send a stamped, self-addressed envelope to: WINNERS LIST c/o MARDEN-KANE, INC., P.O. BOX 701, SAYREVILLE, NJ 08871. Winners Lists will be fulfilled after the May 30, 1992 drawing date.

If Sweepstakes entry form is missing, please print your name and address on a 3"×5" piece of plain paper and send to:

In the U.S.
Harlequin's WISHBOOK Sweepstakes
P.O. Box 1867
Buffalo, NY 14269-1867

In Canada
Harlequin's WISHBOOK Sweepstakes
P.O. Box 609
Fort Erie, Ontario
L2A 5X3

Offer limited to one per household.

© 1990 Harlequin Enterprises Limited   Printed in the U.S.A.

LTY-H890

COMING SOON...

For years Harlequin and Silhouette novels have been taking readers places—but only in their imaginations.

This fall look for PASSPORT TO ROMANCE, a promotion that could take you around the corner or around the world!

Watch for it in September!

★